KRYPTO
The SUPERDOG ™

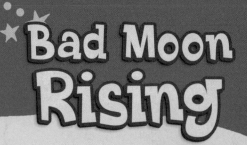

Bad Moon Rising

JESSE LEON MCCANN...................................WRITER
MIN. S. KU ....PENCILLER
JEFF ALBRECHT ....INKER
DAVE TANGUAY ....COLORIST
DAVE TANGUAY ....LETTERER

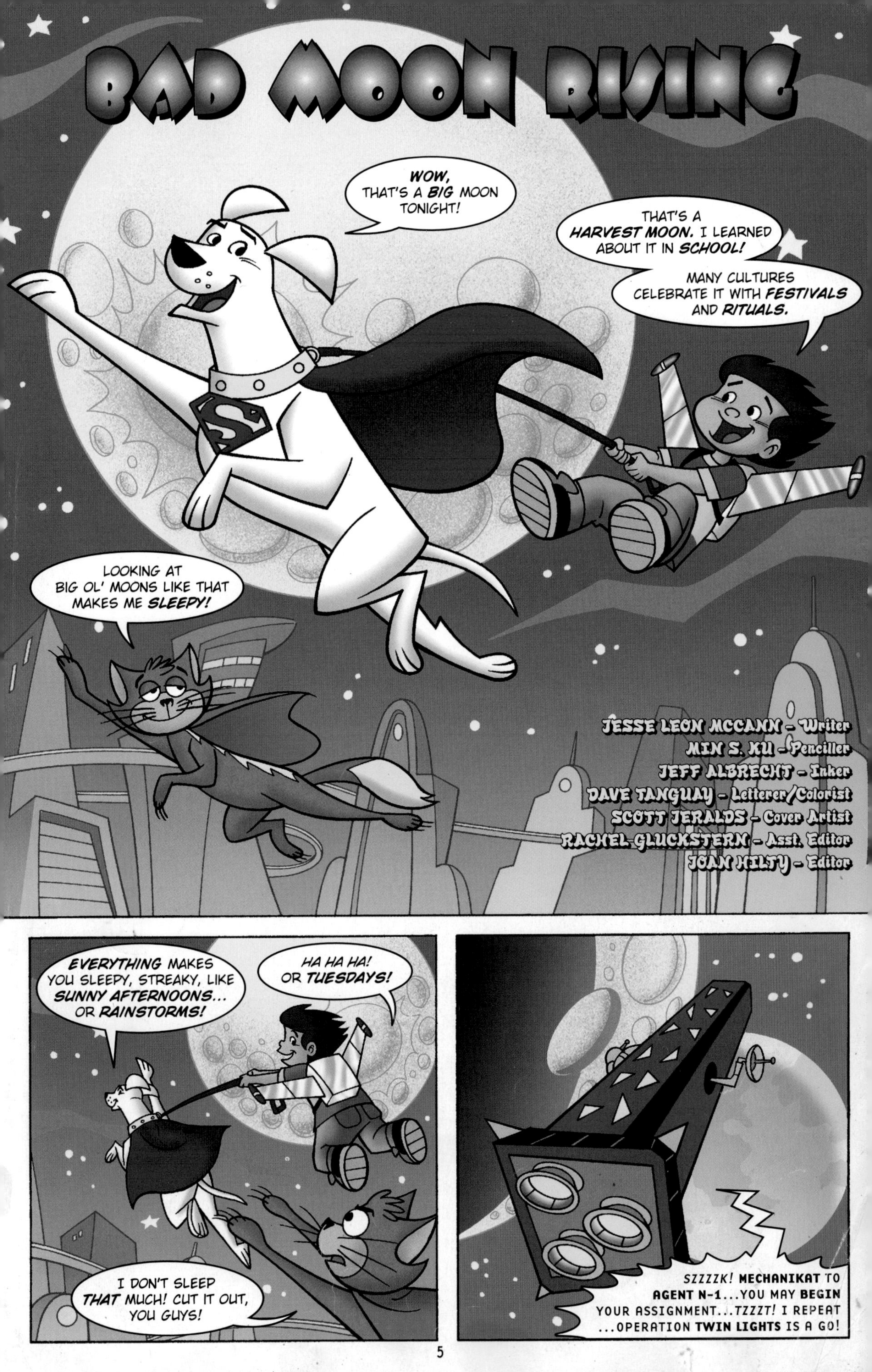
BAD MOON RISING
WOW, THAT'S A BIG MOON TONIGHT!
THAT'S A HARVEST MOON. I LEARNED ABOUT IT IN SCHOOL!
MANY CULTURES CELEBRATE IT WITH FESTIVALS AND RITUALS.
LOOKING AT BIG OL' MOONS LIKE THAT MAKES ME SLEEPY!
JESSE LEON MCCANN - Writer
MIN S. KU - Penciller
JEFF ALBRECHT - Inker
DAVE TANGUAY - Letterer/Colorist
SCOTT JERALDS - Cover Artist
RACHEL GLUCKSTERN - Asst. Editor
JOAN HILTY - Editor
EVERYTHING MAKES YOU SLEEPY, STREAKY, LIKE SUNNY AFTERNOONS... OR RAINSTORMS!
HA HA HA! OR TUESDAYS!
I DON'T SLEEP THAT MUCH! CUT IT OUT, YOU GUYS!
SZZZZK! MECHANIKAT TO AGENT N-1...YOU MAY BEGIN YOUR ASSIGNMENT...TZZZT! I REPEAT ...OPERATION TWIN LIGHTS IS A GO!

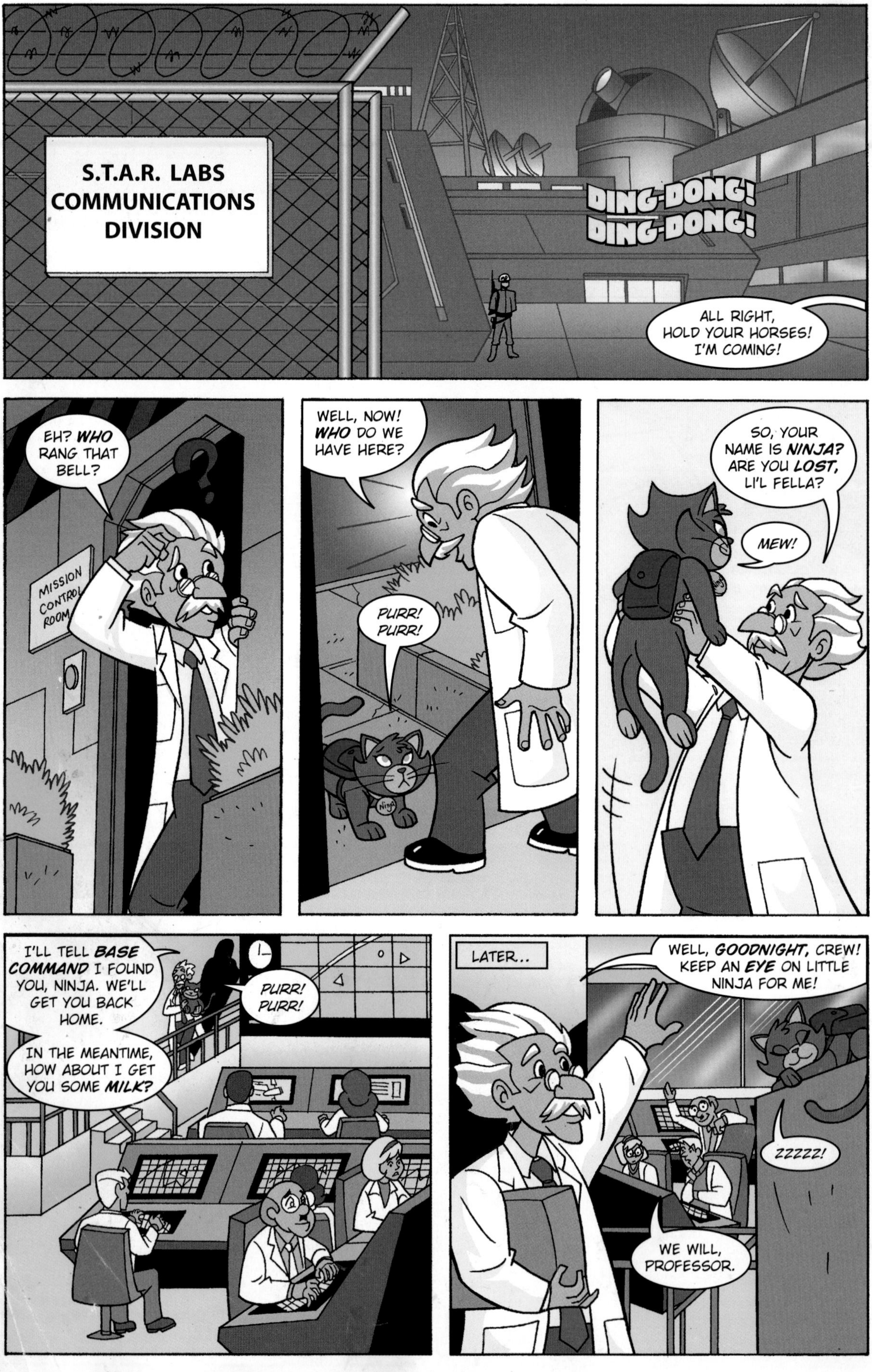
S.T.A.R. LABS
COMMUNICATIONS
DIVISION
DING-DONG!
DING-DONG!
ALL RIGHT, HOLD YOUR HORSES! I'M COMING!
EH? WHO RANG THAT BELL?
MISSION CONTROL ROOM
WELL, NOW! WHO DO WE HAVE HERE?
PURR! PURR!
SO, YOUR NAME IS NINJA? ARE YOU LOST, LI'L FELLA?
MEW!
I'LL TELL BASE COMMAND I FOUND YOU, NINJA. WE'LL GET YOU BACK HOME.
IN THE MEANTIME, HOW ABOUT I GET YOU SOME MILK?
PURR! PURR!
LATER...
WELL, GOODNIGHT, CREW! KEEP AN EYE ON LITTLE NINJA FOR ME!
ZZZZZ!
WE WILL, PROFESSOR.

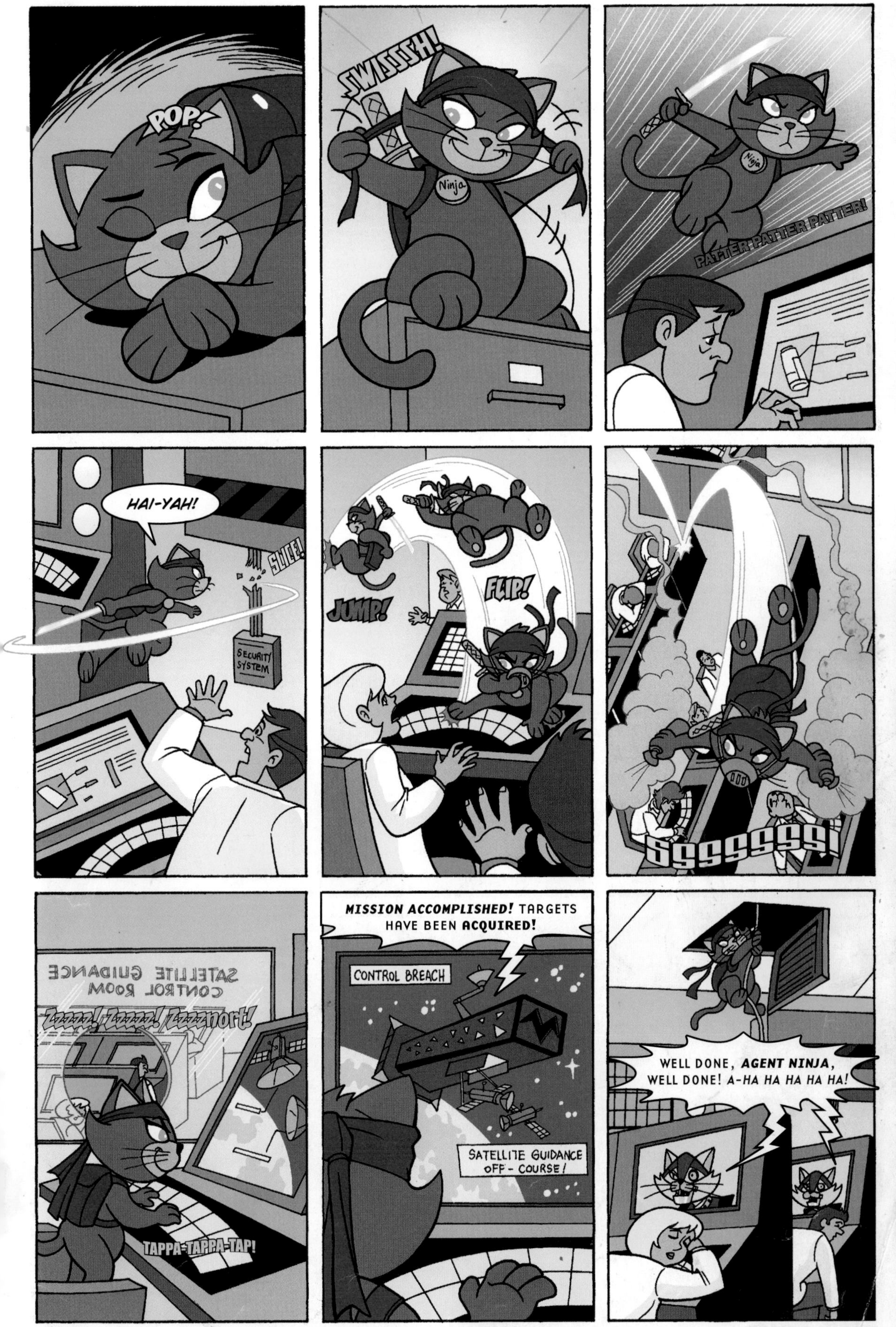
POP!
SWISSSH!
PATTER PATTER PATTER!
HAI-YAH!
SLICE!
SECURITY SYSTEM
JUMP!
FLIP!
SSSSSSS!
SATELLITE GUIDANCE CONTROL ROOM
Zzzzzz! Zzzzzz! Zzzznort!
TAPPA-TAPPA-TAP!
MISSION ACCOMPLISHED! TARGETS HAVE BEEN ACQUIRED!
CONTROL BREACH
SATELLITE GUIDANCE OFF-COURSE!
WELL DONE, AGENT NINJA, WELL DONE! A-HA HA HA HA HA!

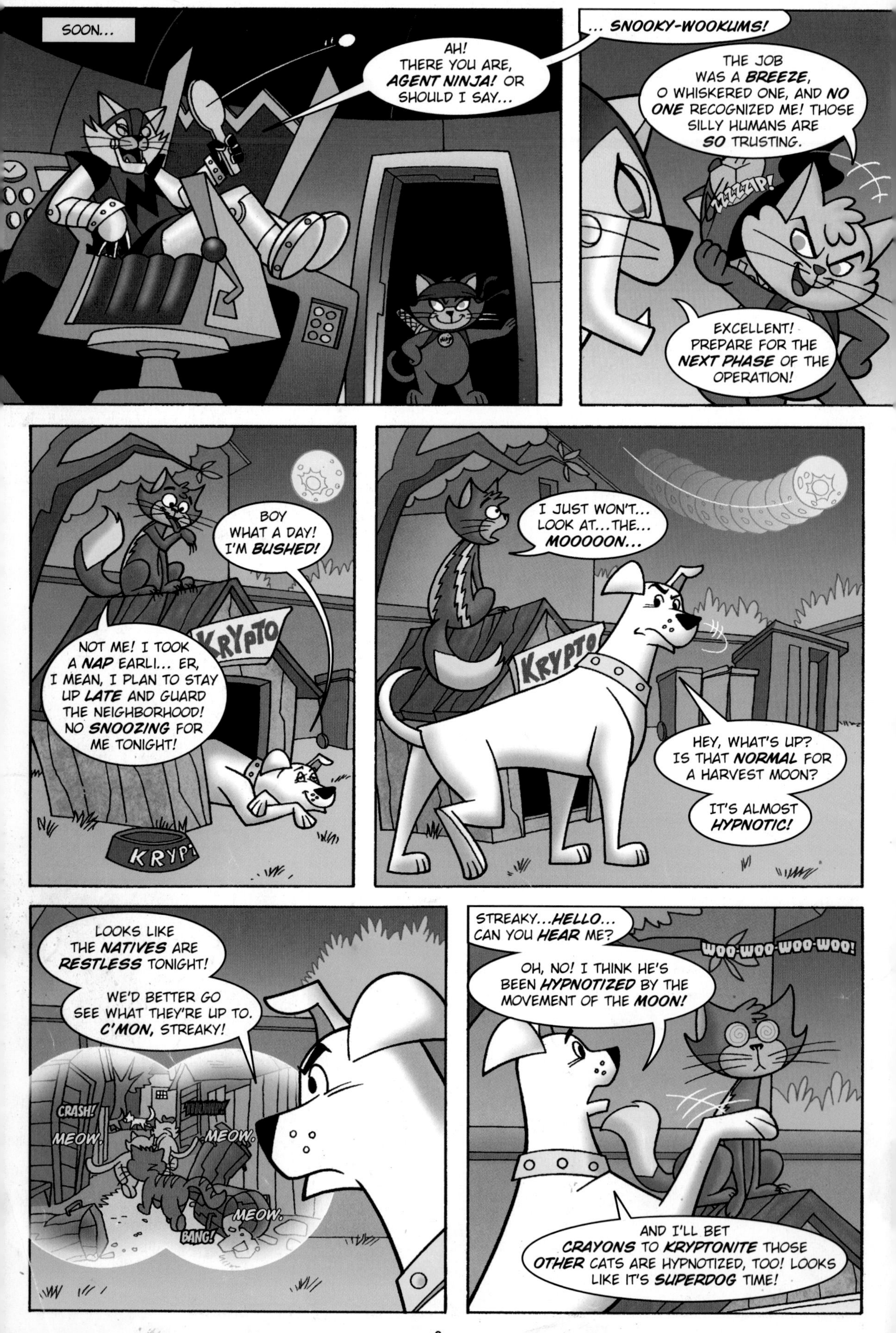

SOON...
AH! THERE YOU ARE, AGENT NINJA! OR SHOULD I SAY...
... SNOOKY-WOOKUMS!
THE JOB WAS A BREEZE, O WHISKERED ONE, AND NO ONE RECOGNIZED ME! THOSE SILLY HUMANS ARE SO TRUSTING.
ZZZZAP!
EXCELLENT! PREPARE FOR THE NEXT PHASE OF THE OPERATION!
BOY WHAT A DAY! I'M BUSHED!
NOT ME! I TOOK A NAP EARLI... ER, I MEAN, I PLAN TO STAY UP LATE AND GUARD THE NEIGHBORHOOD! NO SNOOZING FOR ME TONIGHT!
KRYPTO
I JUST WON'T... LOOK AT...THE... MOOOOON...
KRYPTO
HEY, WHAT'S UP? IS THAT NORMAL FOR A HARVEST MOON?
IT'S ALMOST HYPNOTIC!
LOOKS LIKE THE NATIVES ARE RESTLESS TONIGHT!
WE'D BETTER GO SEE WHAT THEY'RE UP TO. C'MON, STREAKY!
CRASH!
MEOW.
MEOW.
MEOW.
BANG!
STREAKY...HELLO... CAN YOU HEAR ME?
WOO-WOO-WOO-WOO!
OH, NO! I THINK HE'S BEEN HYPNOTIZED BY THE MOVEMENT OF THE MOON!
AND I'LL BET CRAYONS TO KRYPTONITE THOSE OTHER CATS ARE HYPNOTIZED, TOO! LOOKS LIKE IT'S SUPERDOG TIME!

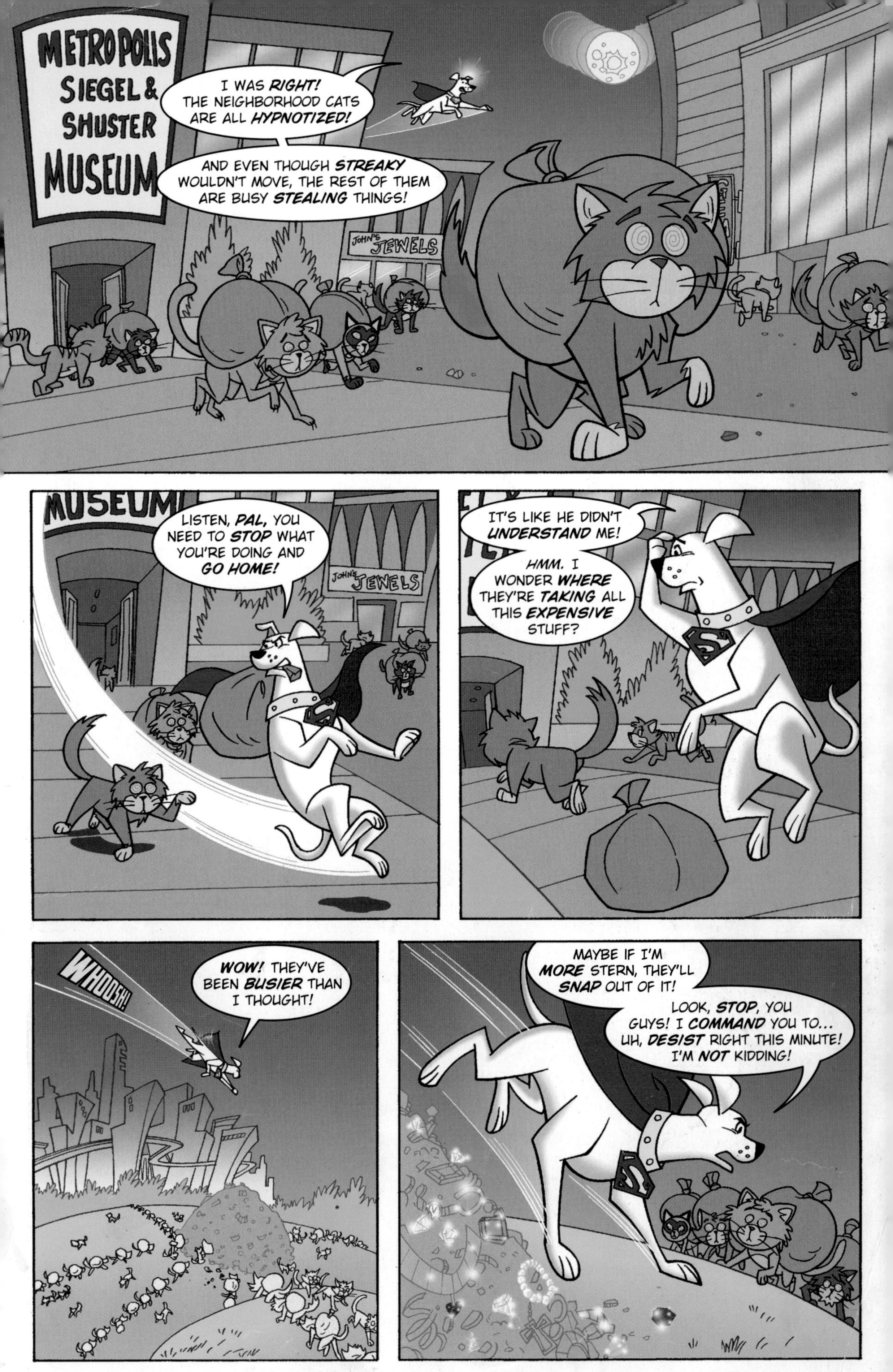
METROPOLIS SIEGEL & SHUSTER MUSEUM
I WAS RIGHT! THE NEIGHBORHOOD CATS ARE ALL HYPNOTIZED!
AND EVEN THOUGH STREAKY WOULDN'T MOVE, THE REST OF THEM ARE BUSY STEALING THINGS!
JOHN'S JEWELS
MUSEUM
LISTEN, PAL, YOU NEED TO STOP WHAT YOU'RE DOING AND GO HOME!
JOHN'S JEWELS
IT'S LIKE HE DIDN'T UNDERSTAND ME!
HMM. I WONDER WHERE THEY'RE TAKING ALL THIS EXPENSIVE STUFF?
WHOOSH!
WOW! THEY'VE BEEN BUSIER THAN I THOUGHT!
MAYBE IF I'M MORE STERN, THEY'LL SNAP OUT OF IT!
LOOK, STOP, YOU GUYS! I COMMAND YOU TO... UH, DESIST RIGHT THIS MINUTE! I'M NOT KIDDING!

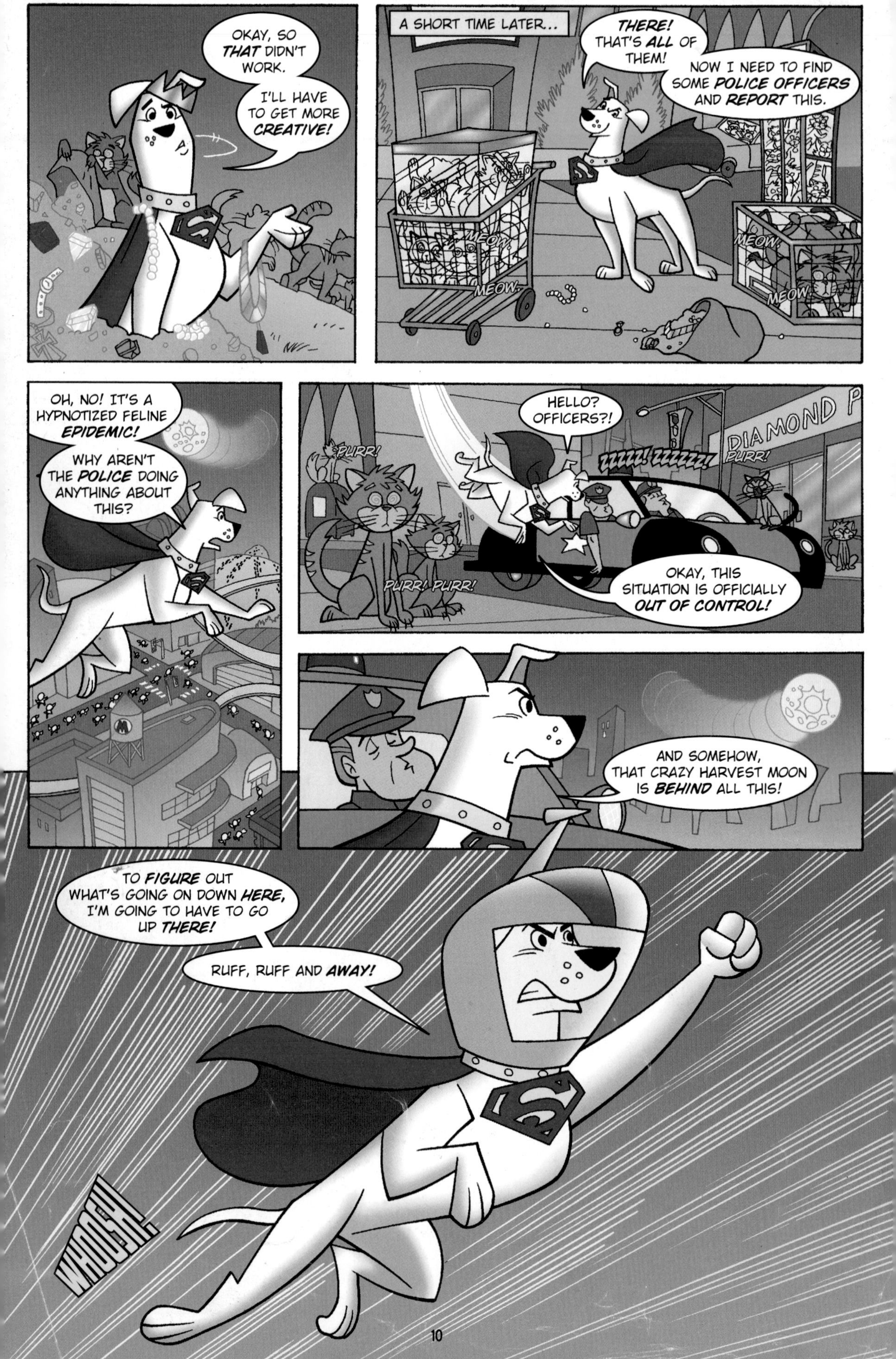
OKAY, SO THAT DIDN'T WORK.
I'LL HAVE TO GET MORE CREATIVE!
A SHORT TIME LATER...
THERE! THAT'S ALL OF THEM!
NOW I NEED TO FIND SOME POLICE OFFICERS AND REPORT THIS.
MEOW.
MEOW.
MEOW.
MEOW.
OH, NO! IT'S A HYPNOTIZED FELINE EPIDEMIC!
WHY AREN'T THE POLICE DOING ANYTHING ABOUT THIS?
HELLO? OFFICERS?!
DIAMOND P
PURR!
ZZZZZZ! ZZZZZZ!
PURR!
PURR! PURR!
OKAY, THIS SITUATION IS OFFICIALLY OUT OF CONTROL!
AND SOMEHOW, THAT CRAZY HARVEST MOON IS BEHIND ALL THIS!
TO FIGURE OUT WHAT'S GOING ON DOWN HERE, I'M GOING TO HAVE TO GO UP THERE!
RUFF, RUFF AND AWAY!
WHOOSH!

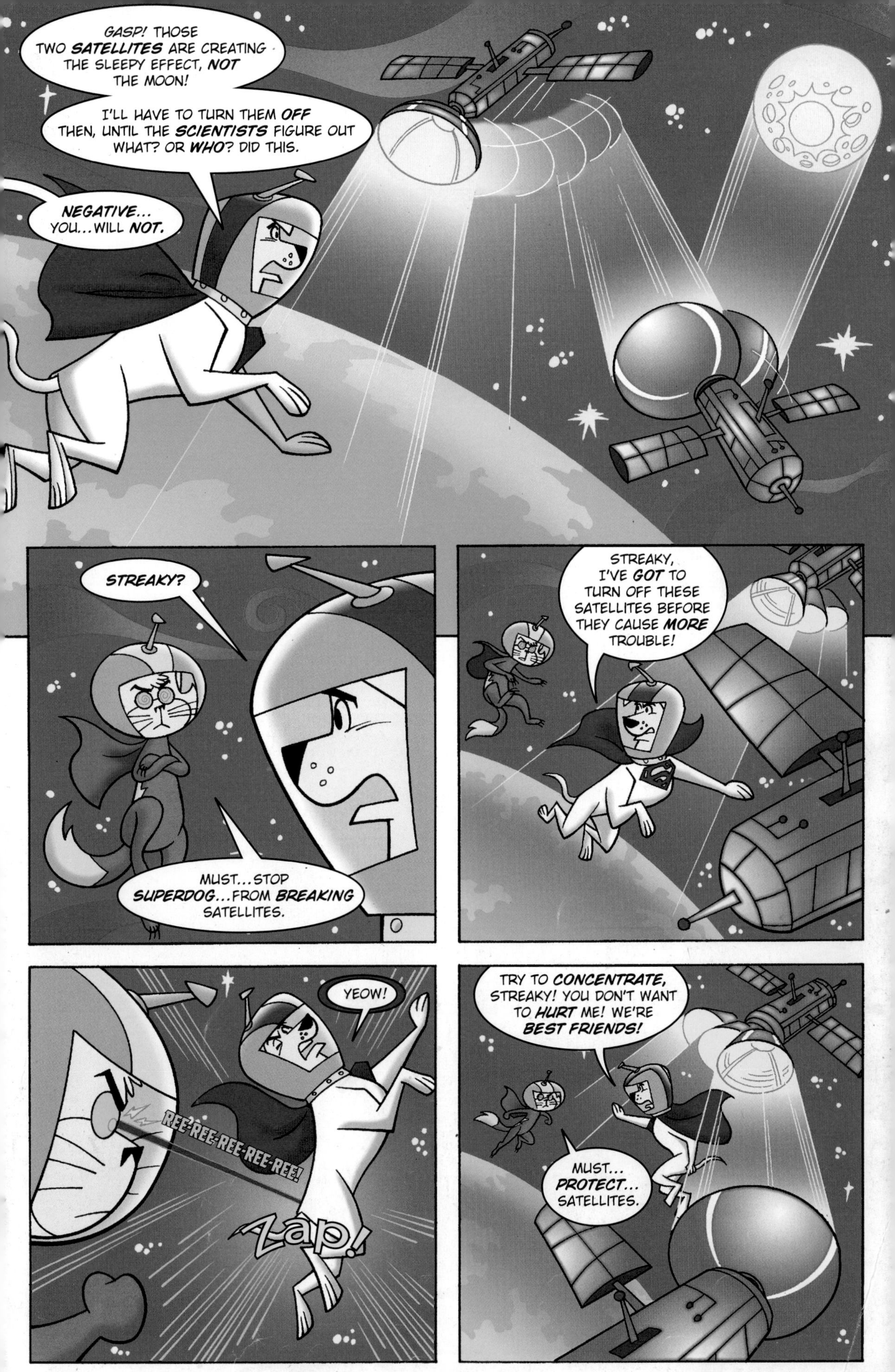
GASP! THOSE TWO SATELLITES ARE CREATING THE SLEEPY EFFECT, NOT THE MOON!
I'LL HAVE TO TURN THEM OFF THEN, UNTIL THE SCIENTISTS FIGURE OUT WHAT? OR WHO? DID THIS.
NEGATIVE... YOU...WILL NOT.
STREAKY?
MUST...STOP SUPERDOG...FROM BREAKING SATELLITES.
STREAKY, I'VE GOT TO TURN OFF THESE SATELLITES BEFORE THEY CAUSE MORE TROUBLE!
YEOW!
REE-REE-REE-REE-REE!
ZAP!
TRY TO CONCENTRATE, STREAKY! YOU DON'T WANT TO HURT ME! WE'RE BEST FRIENDS!
MUST... PROTECT... SATELLITES.

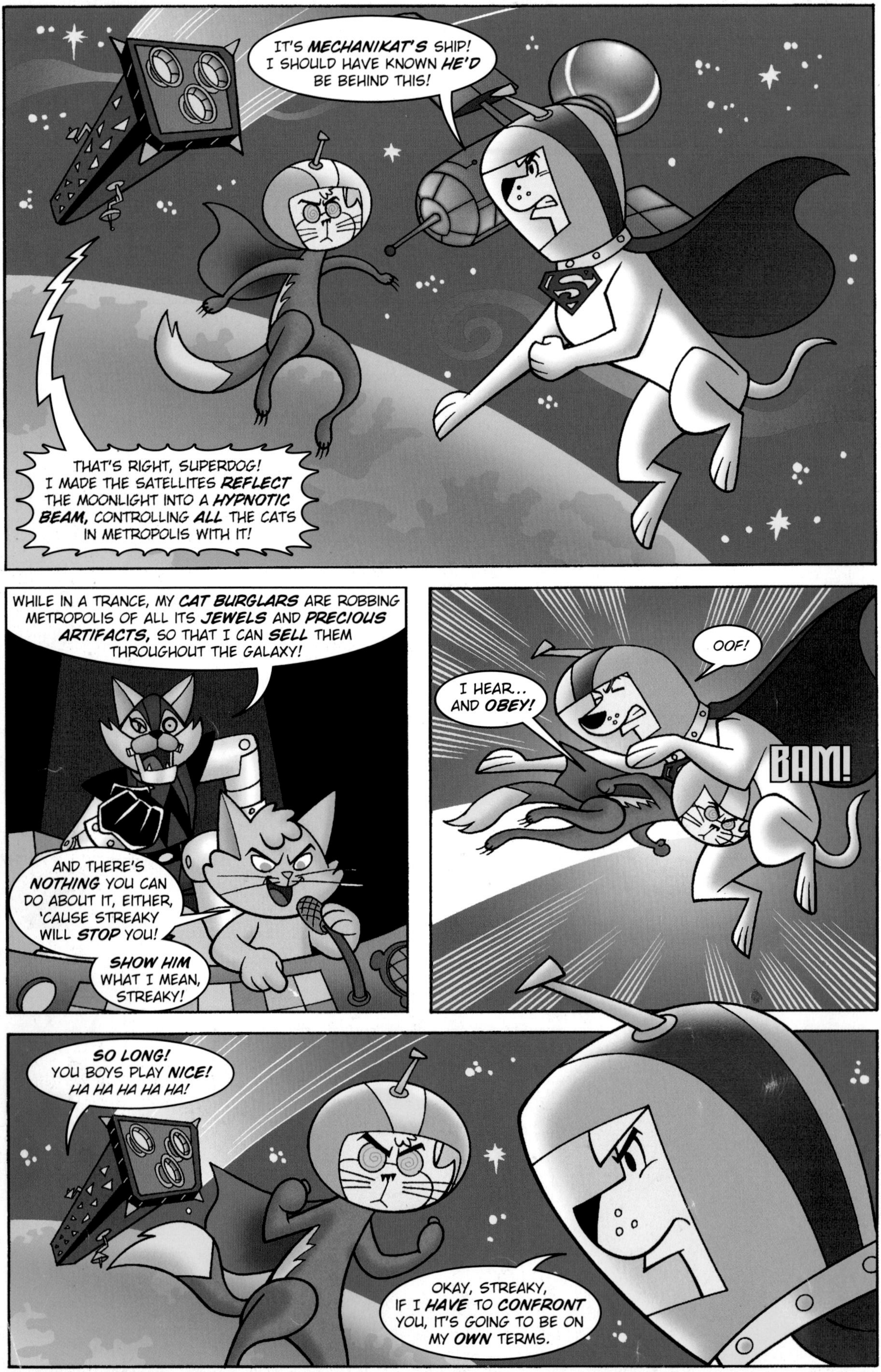
IT'S MECHANIKAT'S SHIP! I SHOULD HAVE KNOWN HE'D BE BEHIND THIS!
THAT'S RIGHT, SUPERDOG! I MADE THE SATELLITES REFLECT THE MOONLIGHT INTO A HYPNOTIC BEAM, CONTROLLING ALL THE CATS IN METROPOLIS WITH IT!
WHILE IN A TRANCE, MY CAT BURGLARS ARE ROBBING METROPOLIS OF ALL ITS JEWELS AND PRECIOUS ARTIFACTS, SO THAT I CAN SELL THEM THROUGHOUT THE GALAXY!
AND THERE'S NOTHING YOU CAN DO ABOUT IT, EITHER, 'CAUSE STREAKY WILL STOP YOU!
SHOW HIM WHAT I MEAN, STREAKY!
I HEAR... AND OBEY!
OOF!
BAM!
SO LONG! YOU BOYS PLAY NICE! HA HA HA HA HA!
OKAY, STREAKY, IF I HAVE TO CONFRONT YOU, IT'S GOING TO BE ON MY OWN TERMS.

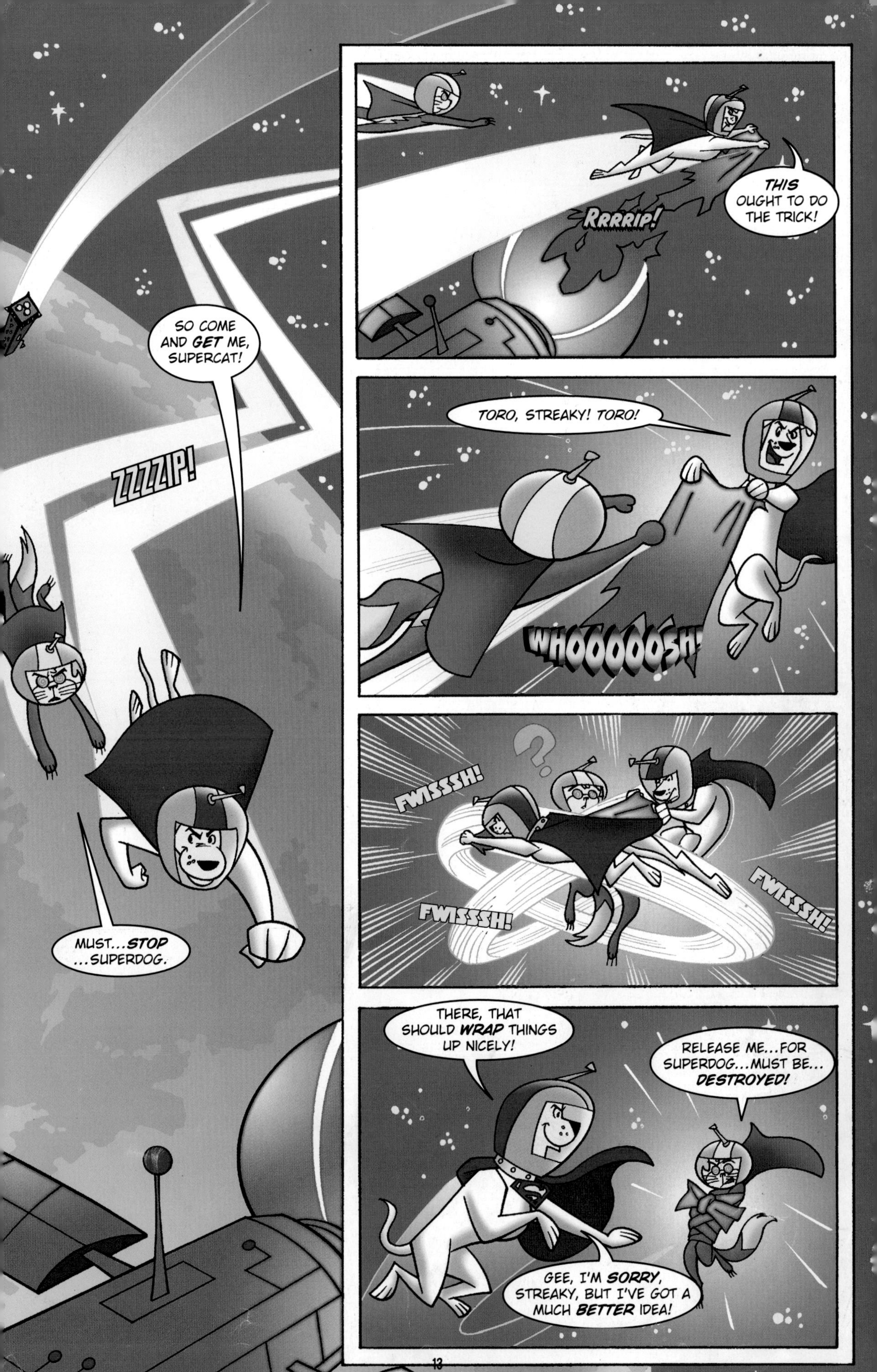
SO COME AND **GET** ME, SUPERCAT!
ZZZZIP!
MUST...**STOP** ...SUPERDOG.
Rrrrip!
THIS OUGHT TO DO THE TRICK!
TORO, STREAKY! TORO!
WHOOOOOOSH!
FWISSSH!
FWISSSH!
FWISSSH!
THERE, THAT SHOULD **WRAP** THINGS UP NICELY!
RELEASE ME...FOR SUPERDOG...MUST BE... **DESTROYED!**
GEE, I'M **SORRY**, STREAKY, BUT I'VE GOT A MUCH **BETTER** IDEA!

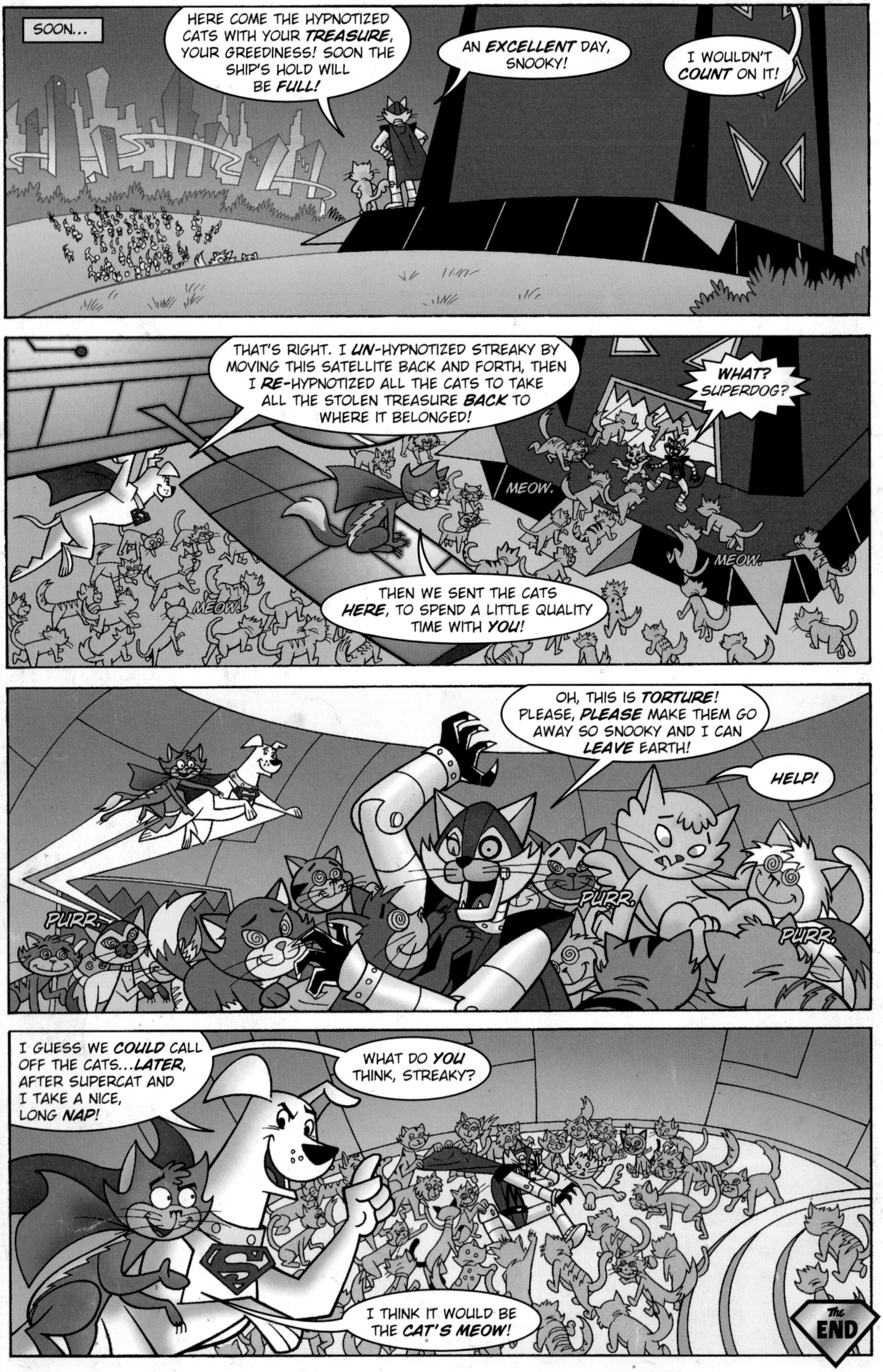
SOON...
HERE COME THE HYPNOTIZED CATS WITH YOUR TREASURE, YOUR GREEDINESS! SOON THE SHIP'S HOLD WILL BE FULL!
AN EXCELLENT DAY, SNOOKY!
I WOULDN'T COUNT ON IT!
THAT'S RIGHT. I UN-HYPNOTIZED STREAKY BY MOVING THIS SATELLITE BACK AND FORTH, THEN I RE-HYPNOTIZED ALL THE CATS TO TAKE ALL THE STOLEN TREASURE BACK TO WHERE IT BELONGED!
WHAT? SUPERDOG?
MEOW.
MEOW.
MEOW!
THEN WE SENT THE CATS HERE, TO SPEND A LITTLE QUALITY TIME WITH YOU!
OH, THIS IS TORTURE! PLEASE, PLEASE MAKE THEM GO AWAY SO SNOOKY AND I CAN LEAVE EARTH!
HELP!
PURR.
PURR.
PURR.
I GUESS WE COULD CALL OFF THE CATS...LATER, AFTER SUPERCAT AND I TAKE A NICE, LONG NAP!
WHAT DO YOU THINK, STREAKY?
I THINK IT WOULD BE THE CAT'S MEOW!
The END

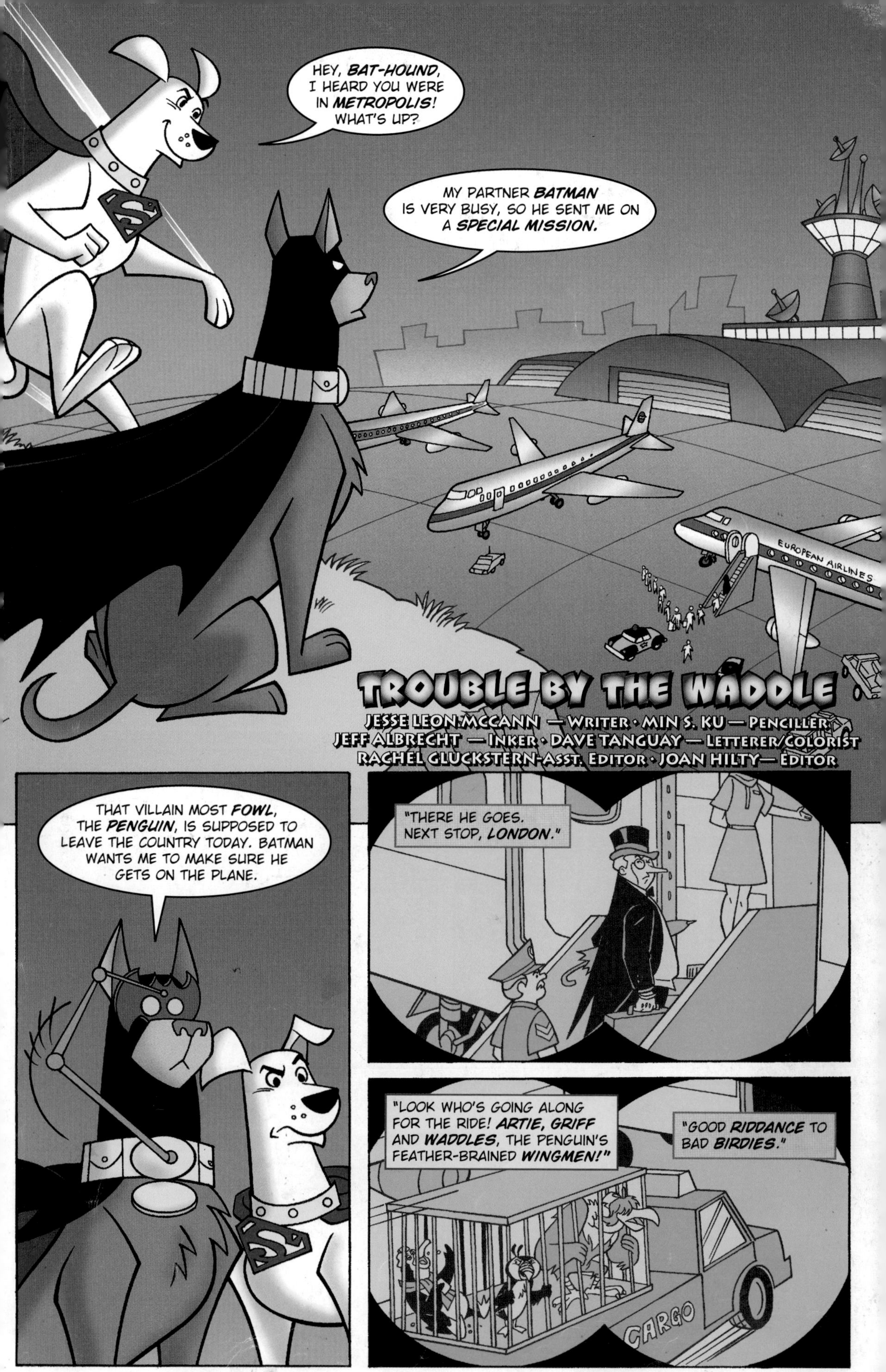
HEY, BAT-HOUND, I HEARD YOU WERE IN METROPOLIS! WHAT'S UP?
MY PARTNER BATMAN IS VERY BUSY, SO HE SENT ME ON A SPECIAL MISSION.
EUROPEAN AIRLINES
TROUBLE BY THE WADDLE
JESSE LEON MCCANN — WRITER · MIN S. KU — PENCILLER
JEFF ALBRECHT — INKER · DAVE TANGUAY — LETTERER/COLORIST
RACHEL GLUCKSTERN-ASST. EDITOR · JOAN HILTY— EDITOR
THAT VILLAIN MOST FOWL, THE PENGUIN, IS SUPPOSED TO LEAVE THE COUNTRY TODAY. BATMAN WANTS ME TO MAKE SURE HE GETS ON THE PLANE.
"THERE HE GOES. NEXT STOP, LONDON."
"LOOK WHO'S GOING ALONG FOR THE RIDE! ARTIE, GRIFF AND WADDLES, THE PENGUIN'S FEATHER-BRAINED WINGMEN!"
"GOOD RIDDANCE TO BAD BIRDIES."
CARGO

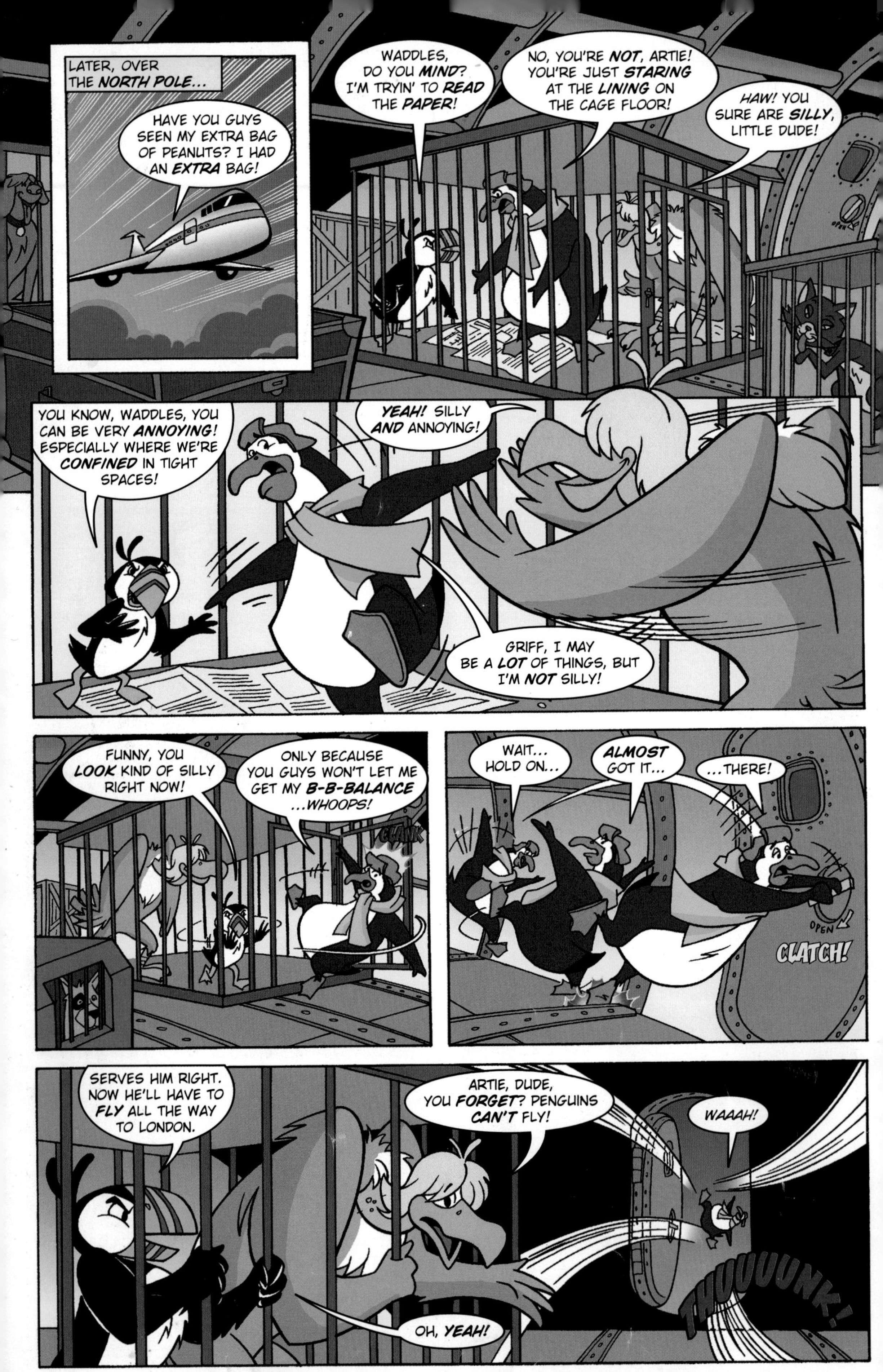
LATER, OVER THE NORTH POLE...
HAVE YOU GUYS SEEN MY EXTRA BAG OF PEANUTS? I HAD AN EXTRA BAG!
WADDLES, DO YOU MIND? I'M TRYIN' TO READ THE PAPER!
NO, YOU'RE NOT, ARTIE! YOU'RE JUST STARING AT THE LINING ON THE CAGE FLOOR!
HAW! YOU SURE ARE SILLY, LITTLE DUDE!
OPEN
YOU KNOW, WADDLES, YOU CAN BE VERY ANNOYING! ESPECIALLY WHERE WE'RE CONFINED IN TIGHT SPACES!
YEAH! SILLY AND ANNOYING!
GRIFF, I MAY BE A LOT OF THINGS, BUT I'M NOT SILLY!
FUNNY, YOU LOOK KIND OF SILLY RIGHT NOW!
ONLY BECAUSE YOU GUYS WON'T LET ME GET MY B-B-BALANCE ...WHOOPS!
CLANK
WAIT... HOLD ON...
ALMOST GOT IT...
...THERE!
OPEN
CLATCH!
SERVES HIM RIGHT. NOW HE'LL HAVE TO FLY ALL THE WAY TO LONDON.
ARTIE, DUDE, YOU FORGET? PENGUINS CAN'T FLY!
WAAAH!
THUUUUNK!
OH, YEAH!

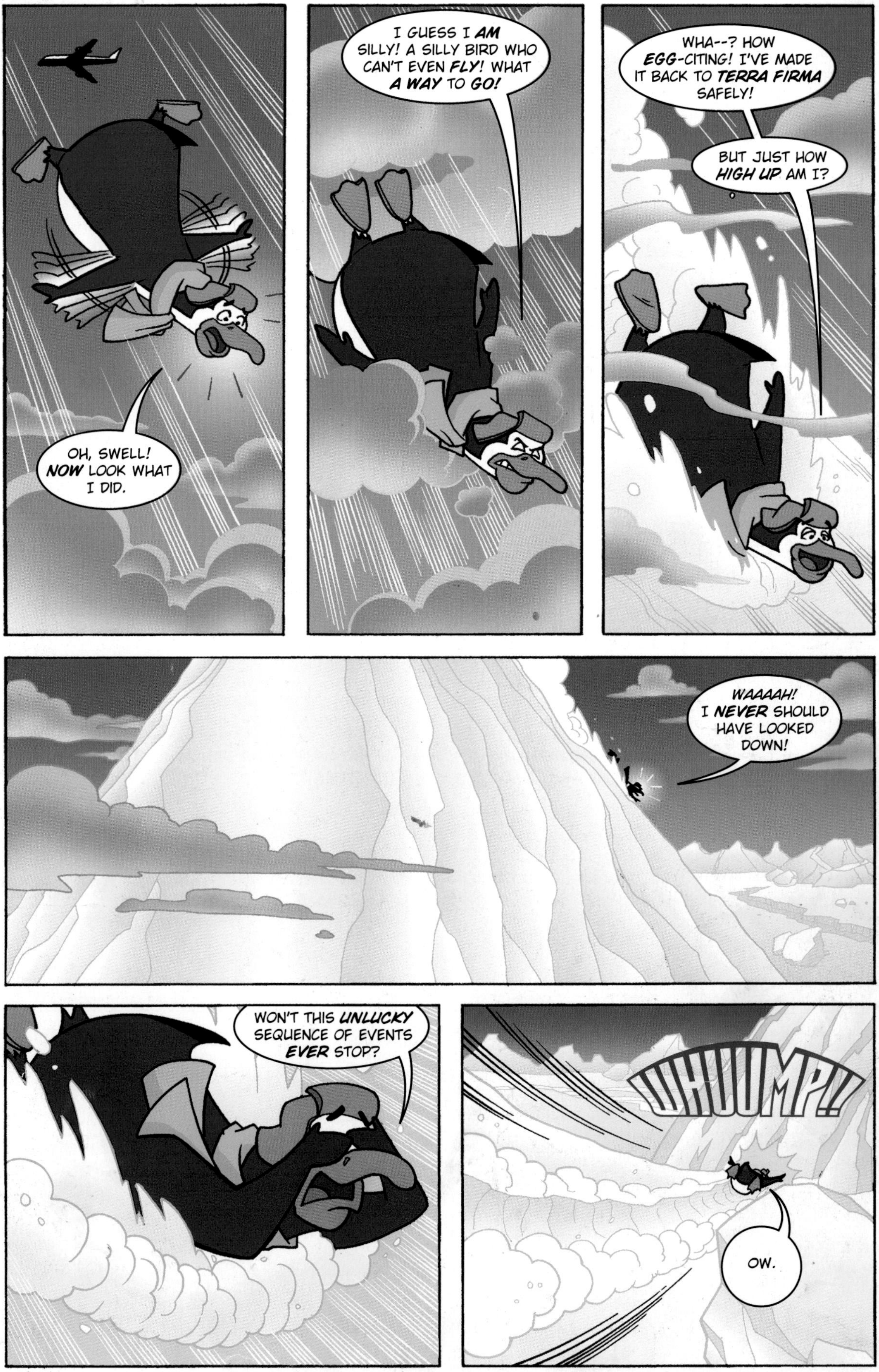
OH, SWELL! NOW LOOK WHAT I DID.
I GUESS I AM SILLY! A SILLY BIRD WHO CAN'T EVEN FLY! WHAT A WAY TO GO!
WHA--? HOW EGG-CITING! I'VE MADE IT BACK TO TERRA FIRMA SAFELY!
BUT JUST HOW HIGH UP AM I?
WAAAAH! I NEVER SHOULD HAVE LOOKED DOWN!
WON'T THIS UNLUCKY SEQUENCE OF EVENTS EVER STOP?
WHUUMP!!
OW.

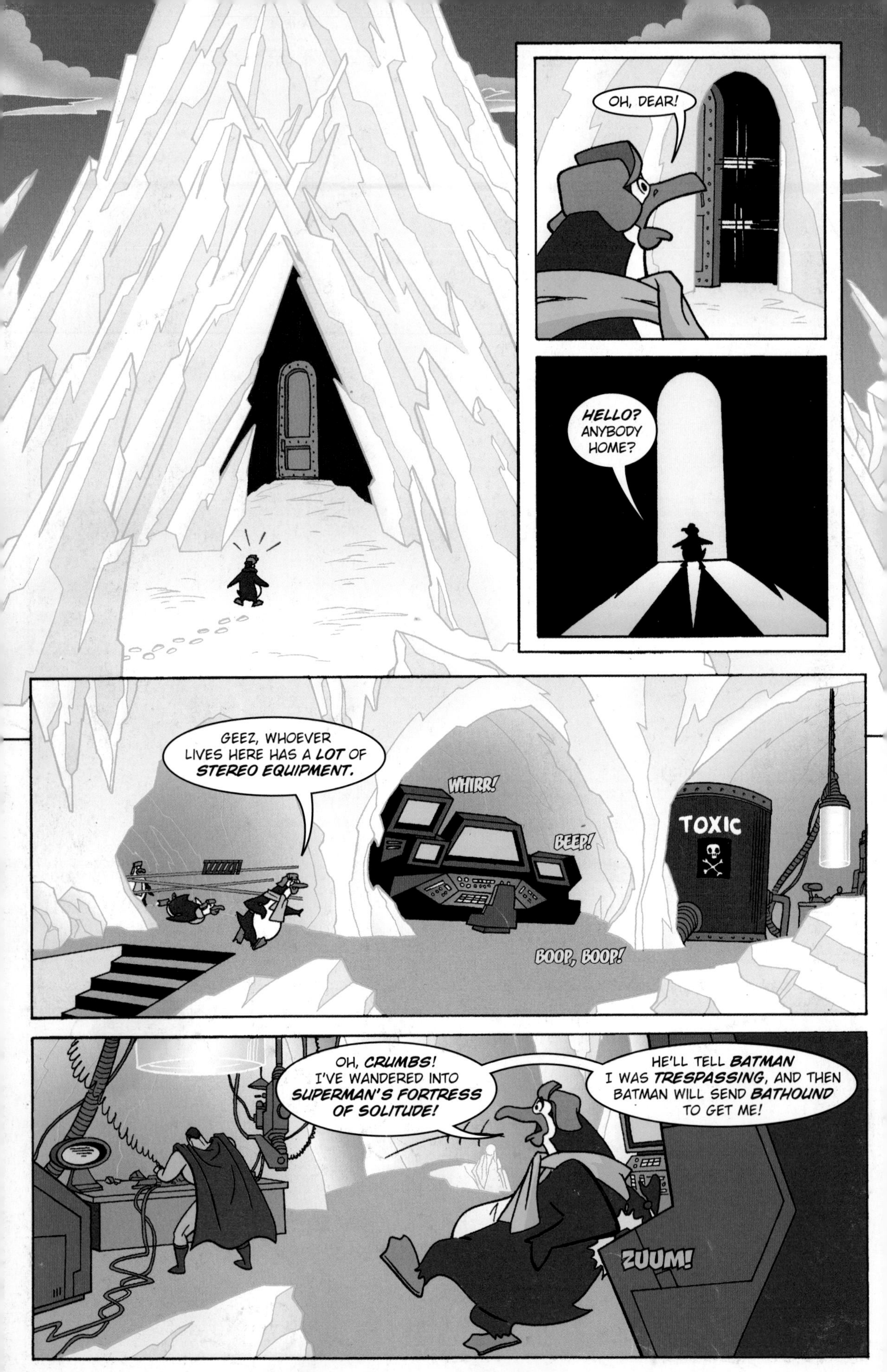
OH, DEAR!
HELLO? ANYBODY HOME?
GEEZ, WHOEVER LIVES HERE HAS A LOT OF STEREO EQUIPMENT.
WHIRR!
BEEP!
TOXIC
BOOP, BOOP!
OH, CRUMBS! I'VE WANDERED INTO SUPERMAN'S FORTRESS OF SOLITUDE!
HE'LL TELL BATMAN I WAS TRESPASSING, AND THEN BATMAN WILL SEND BATHOUND TO GET ME!
ZUUM!

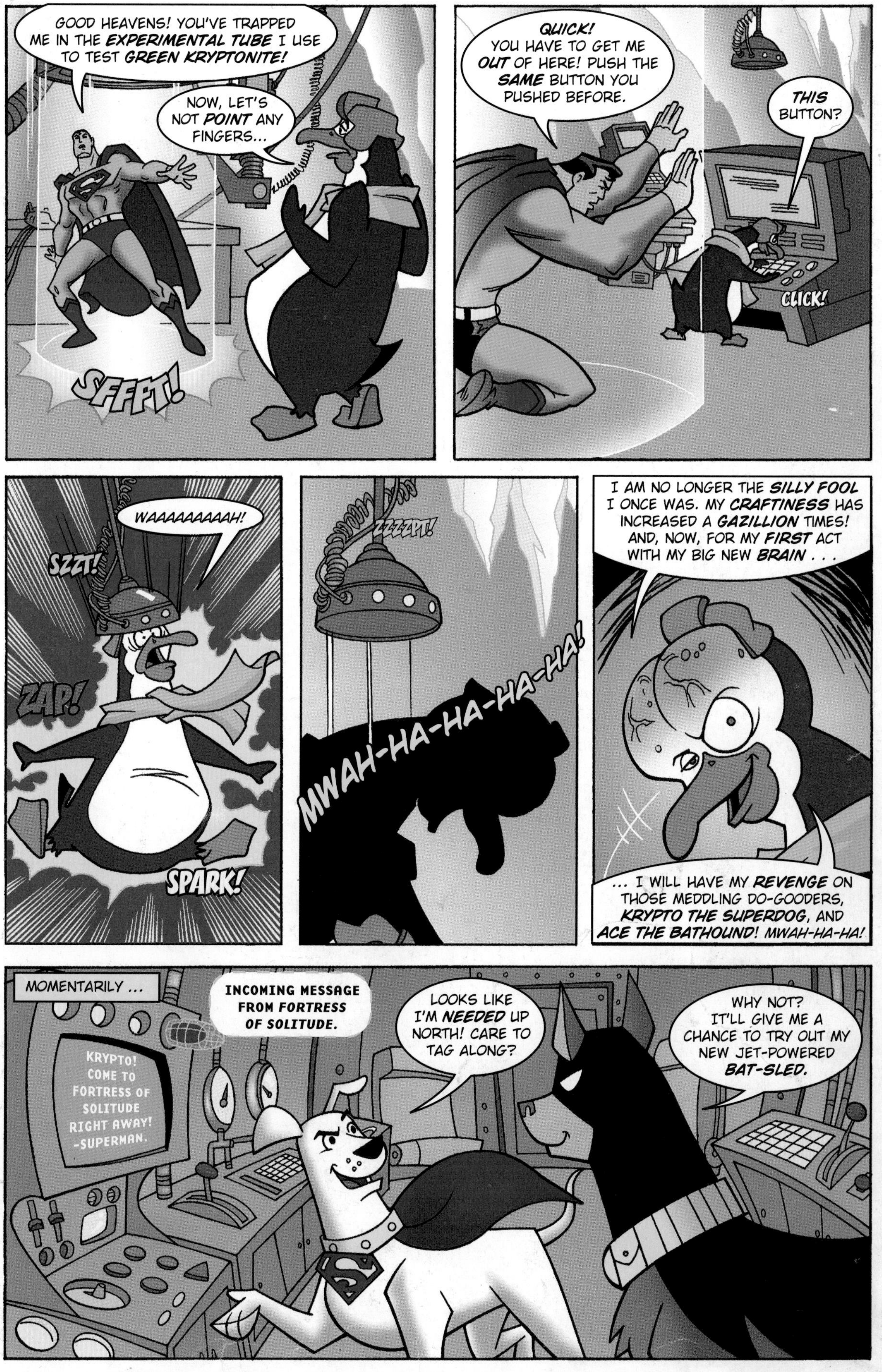
GOOD HEAVENS! YOU'VE TRAPPED ME IN THE EXPERIMENTAL TUBE I USE TO TEST GREEN KRYPTONITE!
NOW, LET'S NOT POINT ANY FINGERS...
SFFFT!
QUICK! YOU HAVE TO GET ME OUT OF HERE! PUSH THE SAME BUTTON YOU PUSHED BEFORE.
THIS BUTTON?
CLICK!
WAAAAAAAAAH!
SZZT!
ZAP!
SPARK!
ZZZZAPT!
MWAH-HA-HA-HA-HA!
I AM NO LONGER THE SILLY FOOL I ONCE WAS. MY CRAFTINESS HAS INCREASED A GAZILLION TIMES! AND, NOW, FOR MY FIRST ACT WITH MY BIG NEW BRAIN . . .
. . . I WILL HAVE MY REVENGE ON THOSE MEDDLING DO-GOODERS, KRYPTO THE SUPERDOG, AND ACE THE BATHOUND! MWAH-HA-HA!
MOMENTARILY . . .
INCOMING MESSAGE FROM FORTRESS OF SOLITUDE.
KRYPTO! COME TO FORTRESS OF SOLITUDE RIGHT AWAY! -SUPERMAN.
LOOKS LIKE I'M NEEDED UP NORTH! CARE TO TAG ALONG?
WHY NOT? IT'LL GIVE ME A CHANCE TO TRY OUT MY NEW JET-POWERED BAT-SLED.

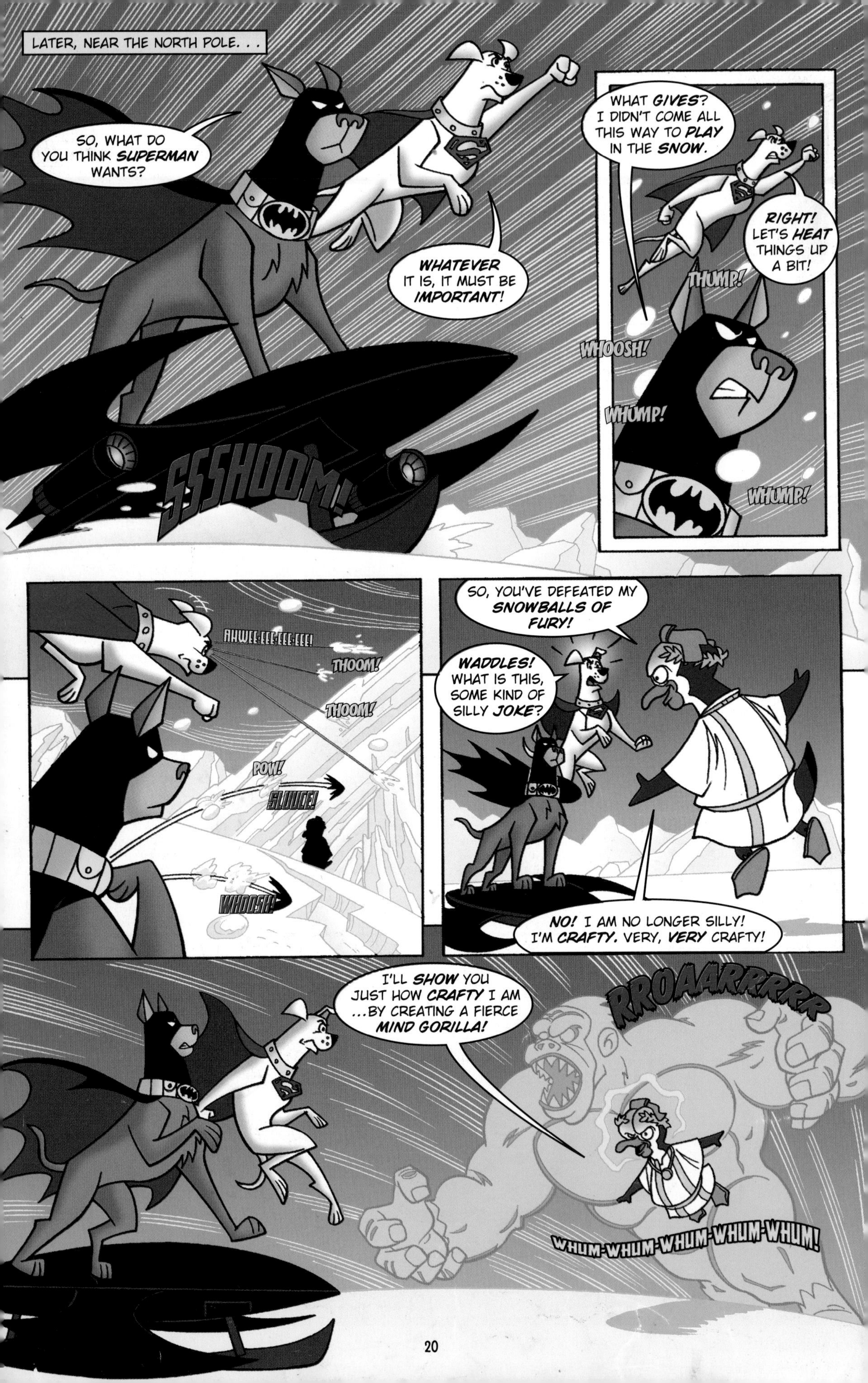

LATER, NEAR THE NORTH POLE. . .
SO, WHAT DO YOU THINK SUPERMAN WANTS?
WHATEVER IT IS, IT MUST BE IMPORTANT!
SSSHOOM!
WHAT GIVES? I DIDN'T COME ALL THIS WAY TO PLAY IN THE SNOW.
RIGHT! LET'S HEAT THINGS UP A BIT!
THUMP!
WHOOSH!
WHUMP!
WHUMP!
AHWEE-EEE-EEE-EEE!
THOOM!
THOOM!
POW!
SLUUCE!
WHOOSH!
SO, YOU'VE DEFEATED MY SNOWBALLS OF FURY!
WADDLES! WHAT IS THIS, SOME KIND OF SILLY JOKE?
NO! I AM NO LONGER SILLY! I'M CRAFTY. VERY, VERY CRAFTY!
I'LL SHOW YOU JUST HOW CRAFTY I AM ...BY CREATING A FIERCE MIND GORILLA!
RROAARRRRR
WHUM-WHUM-WHUM-WHUM-WHUM!

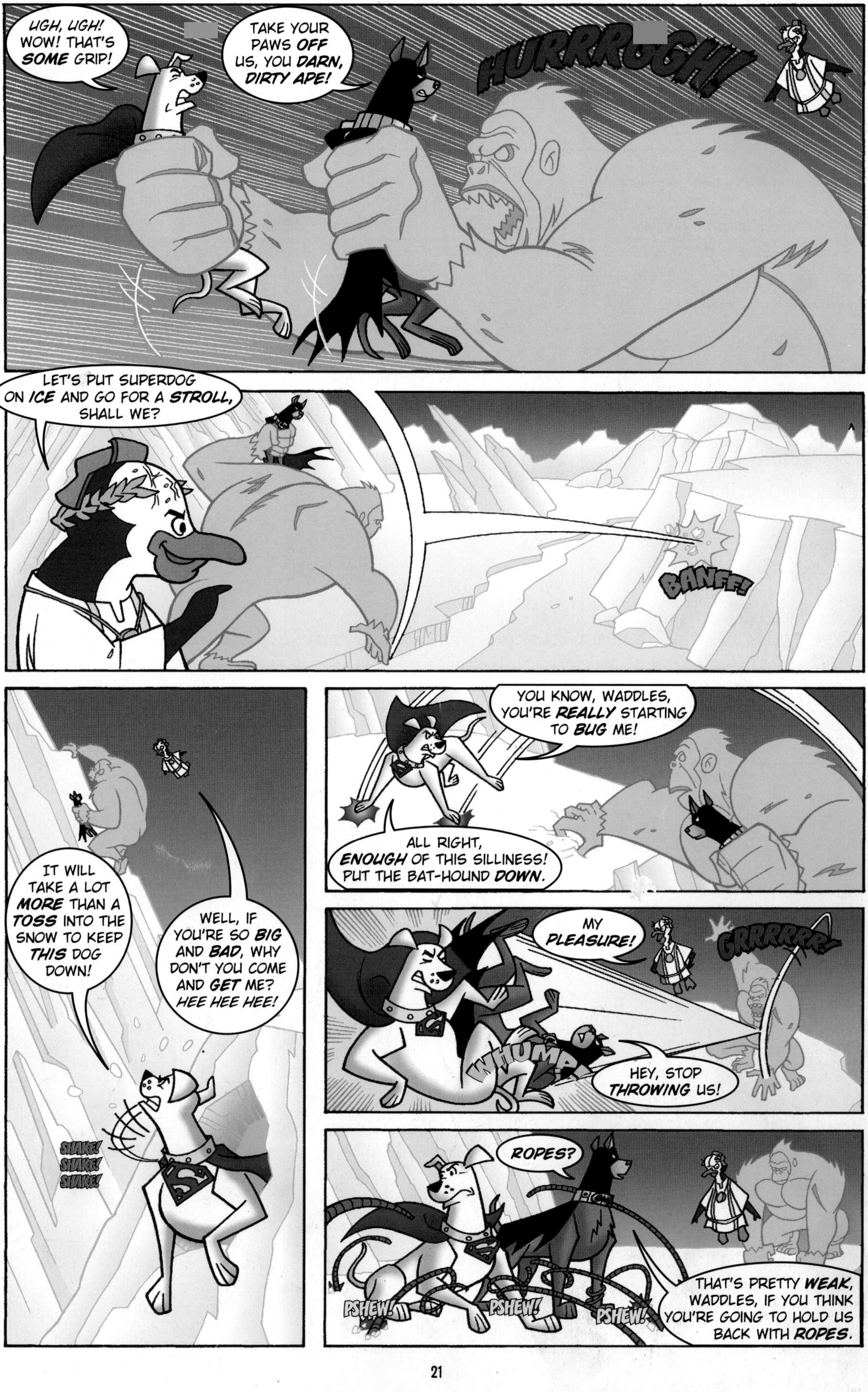
UGH, UGH! WOW! THAT'S SOME GRIP!
TAKE YOUR PAWS OFF US, YOU DARN, DIRTY APE!
HURRRGGH!
LET'S PUT SUPERDOG ON ICE AND GO FOR A STROLL, SHALL WE?
BANFF!
IT WILL TAKE A LOT MORE THAN A TOSS INTO THE SNOW TO KEEP THIS DOG DOWN!
WELL, IF YOU'RE SO BIG AND BAD, WHY DON'T YOU COME AND GET ME? HEE HEE HEE!
SHAKE! SHAKE! SHAKE!
YOU KNOW, WADDLES, YOU'RE REALLY STARTING TO BUG ME!
ALL RIGHT, ENOUGH OF THIS SILLINESS! PUT THE BAT-HOUND DOWN.
MY PLEASURE!
GRRRRRR!
WHUMP!
HEY, STOP THROWING US!
ROPES?
PSHEW! PSHEW! PSHEW!
THAT'S PRETTY WEAK, WADDLES, IF YOU THINK YOU'RE GOING TO HOLD US BACK WITH ROPES.

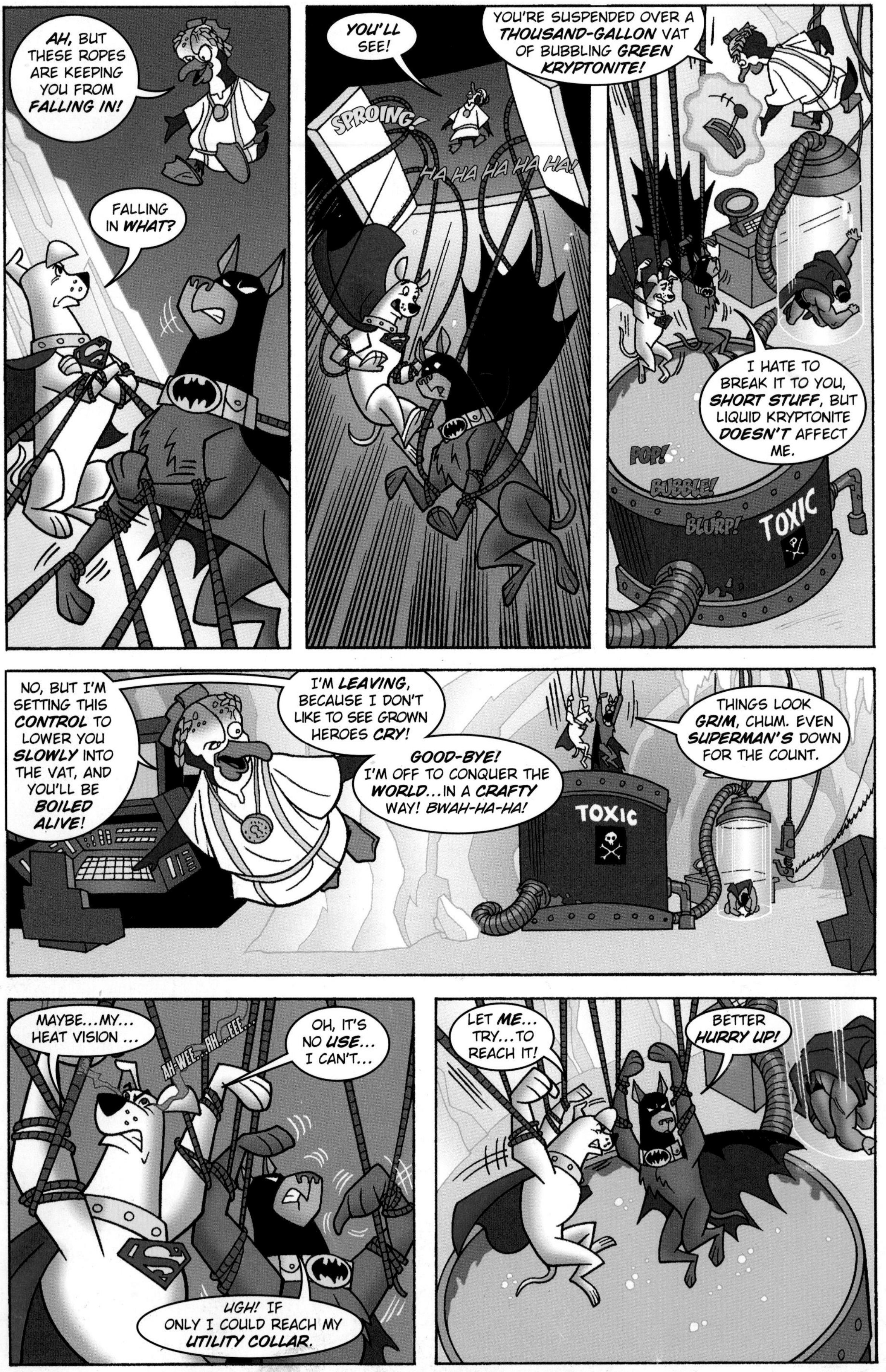
AH, BUT THESE ROPES ARE KEEPING YOU FROM FALLING IN!
FALLING IN WHAT?
YOU'LL SEE!
SPROING!
HA HA HA HA HA!
YOU'RE SUSPENDED OVER A THOUSAND-GALLON VAT OF BUBBLING GREEN KRYPTONITE!
I HATE TO BREAK IT TO YOU, SHORT STUFF, BUT LIQUID KRYPTONITE DOESN'T AFFECT ME.
POP!
BUBBLE!
BLURP!
TOXIC
NO, BUT I'M SETTING THIS CONTROL TO LOWER YOU SLOWLY INTO THE VAT, AND YOU'LL BE BOILED ALIVE!
I'M LEAVING, BECAUSE I DON'T LIKE TO SEE GROWN HEROES CRY!
GOOD-BYE! I'M OFF TO CONQUER THE WORLD...IN A CRAFTY WAY! BWAH-HA-HA!
TOXIC
THINGS LOOK GRIM, CHUM. EVEN SUPERMAN'S DOWN FOR THE COUNT.
MAYBE...MY... HEAT VISION ...
AH-WEE...AH...EEE...
OH, IT'S NO USE... I CAN'T...
UGH! IF ONLY I COULD REACH MY UTILITY COLLAR.
LET ME... TRY...TO REACH IT!
BETTER HURRY UP!

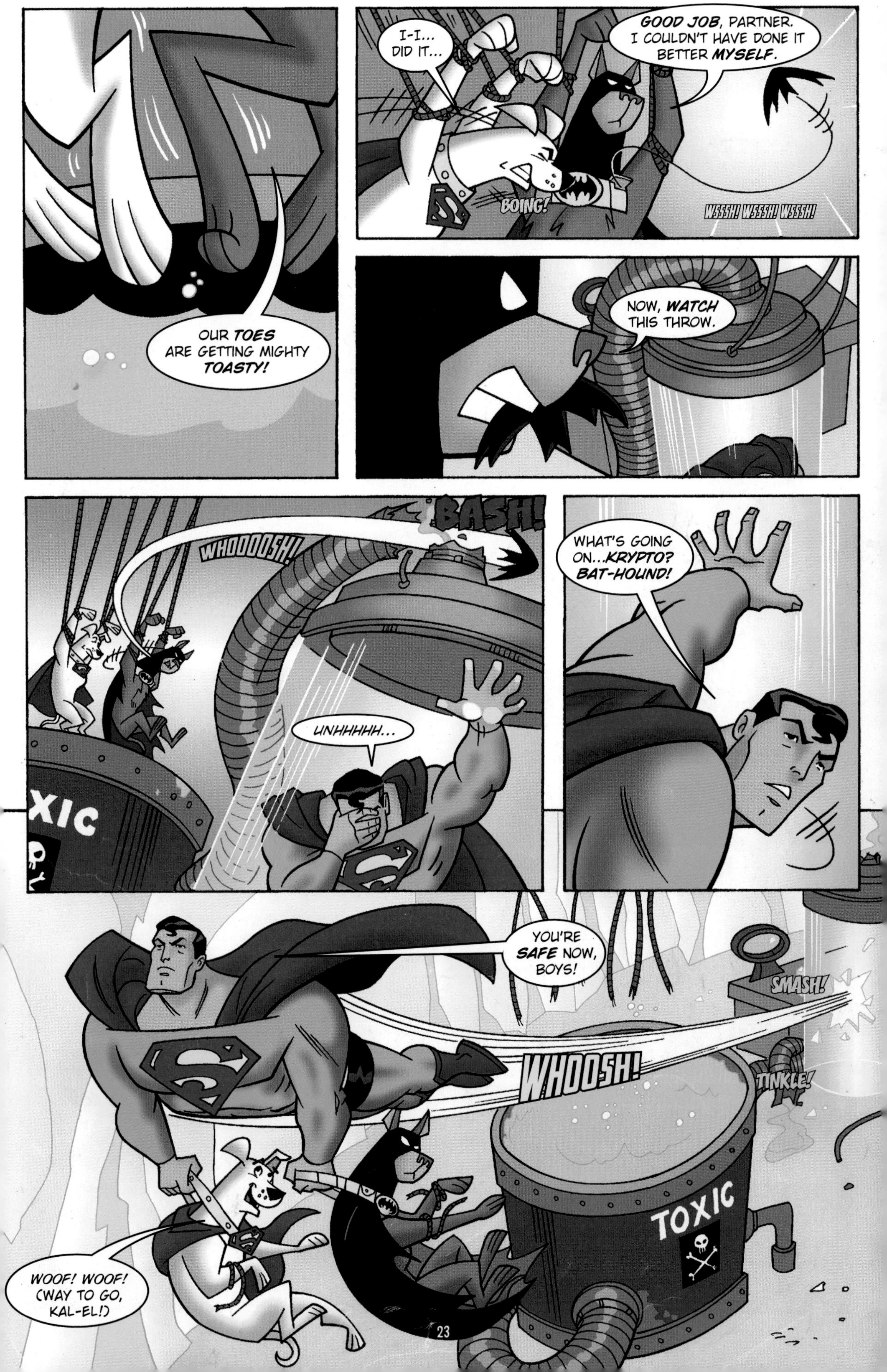
OUR TOES ARE GETTING MIGHTY TOASTY!
I-I... DID IT...
GOOD JOB, PARTNER. I COULDN'T HAVE DONE IT BETTER MYSELF.
BOING!
WSSSH! WSSSH! WSSSH!
NOW, WATCH THIS THROW.
BASH!
WHOOOOSH!
UNHHHHH...
XIC
WHAT'S GOING ON...KRYPTO? BAT-HOUND!
YOU'RE SAFE NOW, BOYS!
SMASH!
WHOOSH!
TINKLE!
TOXIC
WOOF! WOOF! (WAY TO GO, KAL-EL!)

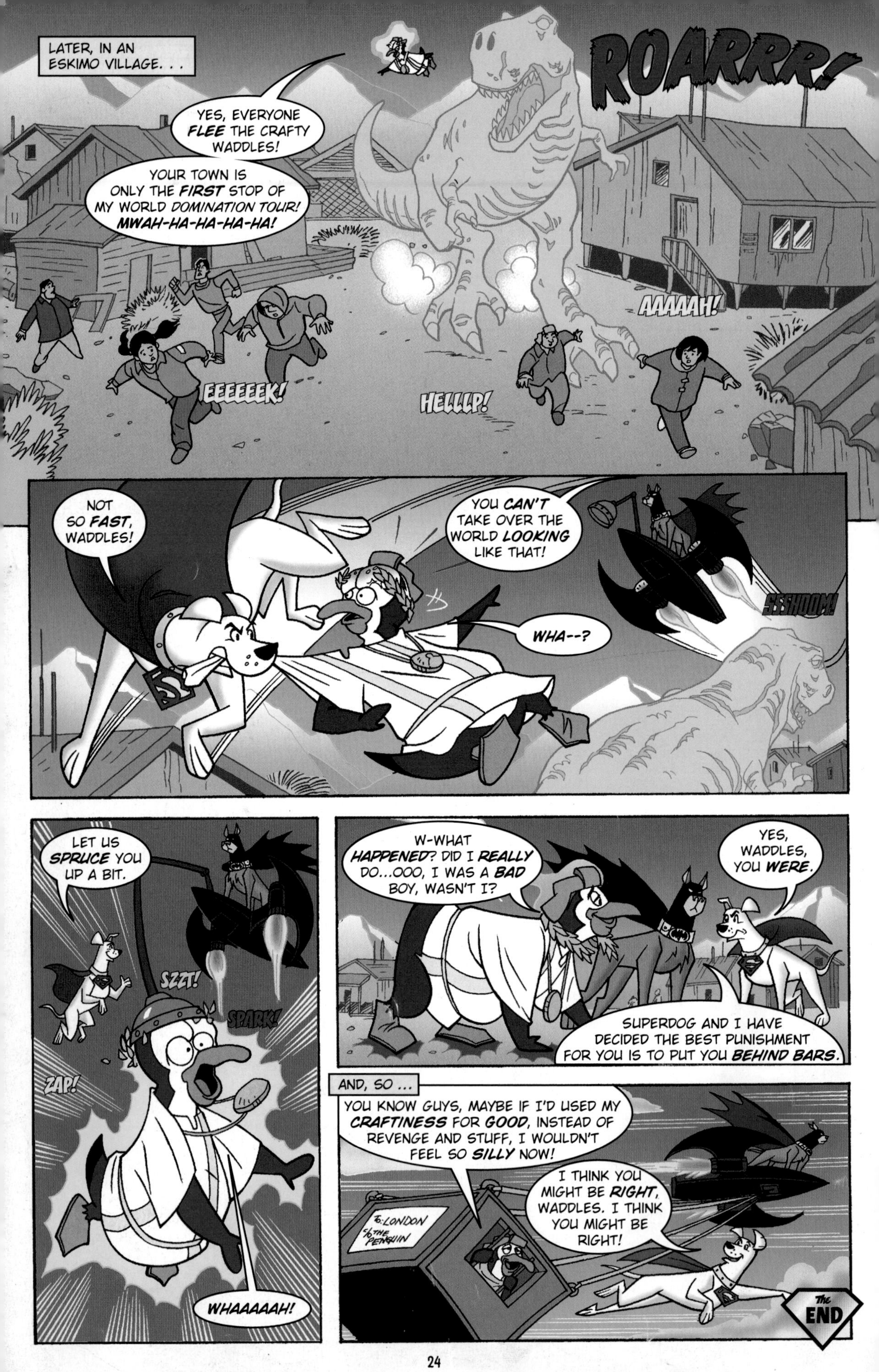

LATER, IN AN ESKIMO VILLAGE. . .
ROARRR!
YES, EVERYONE FLEE THE CRAFTY WADDLES!
YOUR TOWN IS ONLY THE FIRST STOP OF MY WORLD DOMINATION TOUR! MWAH-HA-HA-HA-HA!
AAAAAH!
EEEEEEK!
HELLLP!
NOT SO FAST, WADDLES!
YOU CAN'T TAKE OVER THE WORLD LOOKING LIKE THAT!
SSHOOM!
WHA--?
LET US SPRUCE YOU UP A BIT.
SZZT!
SPARK!
ZAP!
WHAAAAAH!
W-WHAT HAPPENED? DID I REALLY DO...OOO, I WAS A BAD BOY, WASN'T I?
YES, WADDLES, YOU WERE.
SUPERDOG AND I HAVE DECIDED THE BEST PUNISHMENT FOR YOU IS TO PUT YOU BEHIND BARS.
AND, SO ...
YOU KNOW GUYS, MAYBE IF I'D USED MY CRAFTINESS FOR GOOD, INSTEAD OF REVENGE AND STUFF, I WOULDN'T FEEL SO SILLY NOW!
TO: LONDON c/o THE PENGUIN
I THINK YOU MIGHT BE RIGHT, WADDLES. I THINK YOU MIGHT BE RIGHT!
The END

Superdog Jokes!

WHAT DO YOU CALL A BOUNCY BREED OF DOG?

A SPRINGER SPANIEL!

WHAT IS THE NAME OF A FAMOUS DOGGY GAME SHOW HOST?

BOB BARKER!

WHAT DID THE WRITER NAME HIS STORY ABOUT A DEPRESSED DOG?

A VERY SAD TAIL.

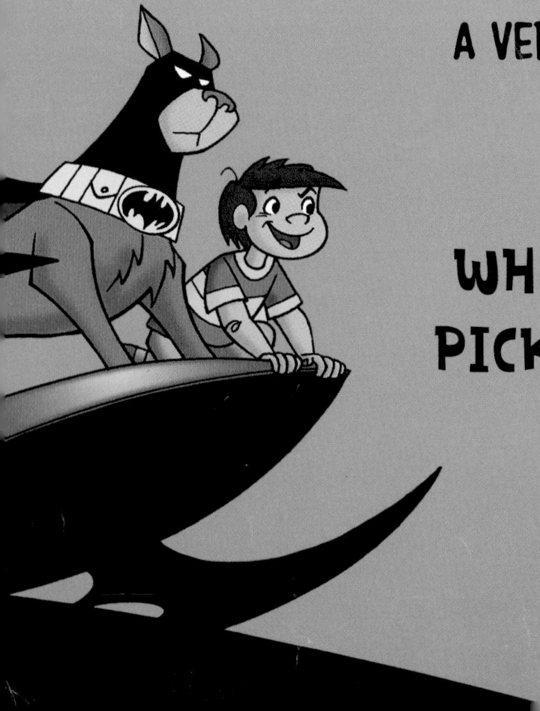

WHAT KIND OF POOCH PICKS ON OTHER PUPS?

A BULLY-DOG!

Creators

JESSE LEON MCCANN WRITER

Jesse Leon McCann is a *New York Times* Top-Ten Children's Book Writer, as well as a prolific all-ages comics writer. His credits include Pinky and the Brain, Animaniacs, and Looney Tunes for DC Comics; Scooby-Doo and Shrek 2 for Scholastic; and The Simpsons and Futurama for Bongo Comics. He lives in Los Angeles with his wife and four cats.

MIN SUNG KU PENCILLER

As a young child, Min Sung Ku dreamed of becoming a comic book illustrator. At six years old, he drew a picture of Superman standing behind the American flag. He has since achieved his childhood dream, having illustrated popular licensed comics properties like the Justice League, Batman Beyond, Spider-Man, Ben 10, Phineas & Ferb, the Replacements, the Proud Family, Krpyto the Superdog, and, of course, Superman. Min lives with his lovely wife and their beautiful twin daughters, Elisia and Eliana.

DAVE TANGUAY COLORIST/LETTERER

David Tanguay has over 20 years of experience in the comic book industry. He has worked as an editor, layout artist, colorist, and letterer. He has also done web design, and he taught computer graphics at the State University of New York.

Glossary

ACQUIRED (uh-KWIRED) – obtained or got something

ARTIFACTS (AR-tuh-faktz) – handmade objects

DESIST (di-SIST) – cease, stop, or give up

HYPNOTIC (hip-NOT-ik) – inducing sleep or a trance

PHASE (FAZE) – a state or step in a process

RESTLESS (REST-liss) – hard to keep still or to concentrate on anything

RITUALS (RICH-oo-uhl) – an action or set of actions that are repeated often

TRANCE (TRANSS) – a mental state in which you are not entirely aware of what is happening around you

TRESPASSING (TRESS-pass-ing) – entering someone's private property without permission

Visual Questions & Prompts

1. EXPLAIN WHAT IS HAPPENING TO STREAKY IN THIS PANEL. WHY DO HIS EYES LOOK THAT WAY?

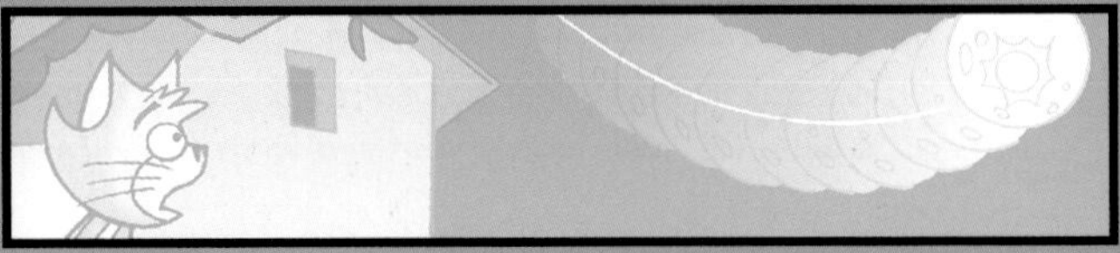

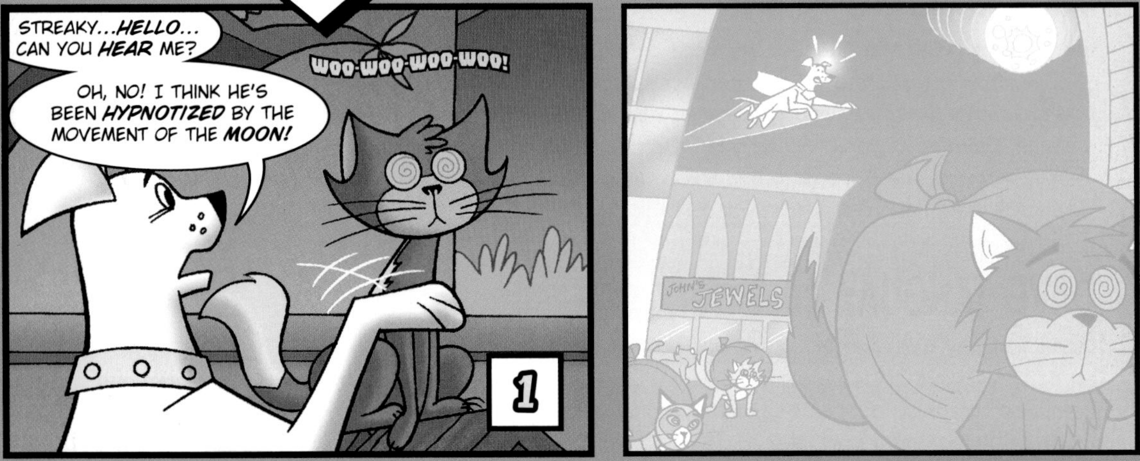
STREAKY...*HELLO*... CAN YOU *HEAR* ME?
WOO-WOO-WOO-WOO!
OH, NO! I THINK HE'S BEEN *HYPNOTIZED* BY THE MOVEMENT OF THE *MOON!*
1
JOHN'S JEWELS

2. KRYPTO AND ACE MAKE A GREAT TEAM. IDENTIFY A FEW OTHER PANELS IN THIS COMIC BOOK WHERE TWO CHARACTERS WORK TOGETHER.

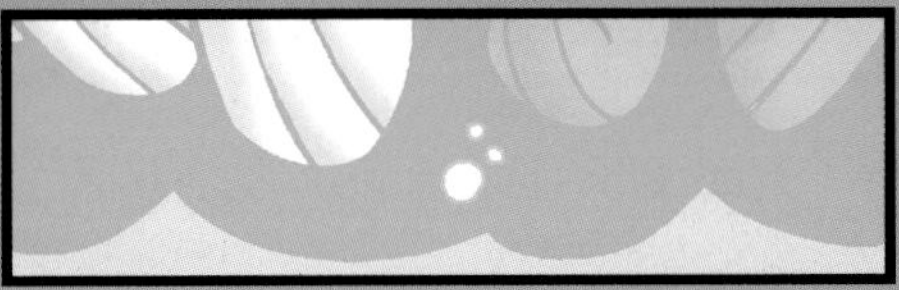

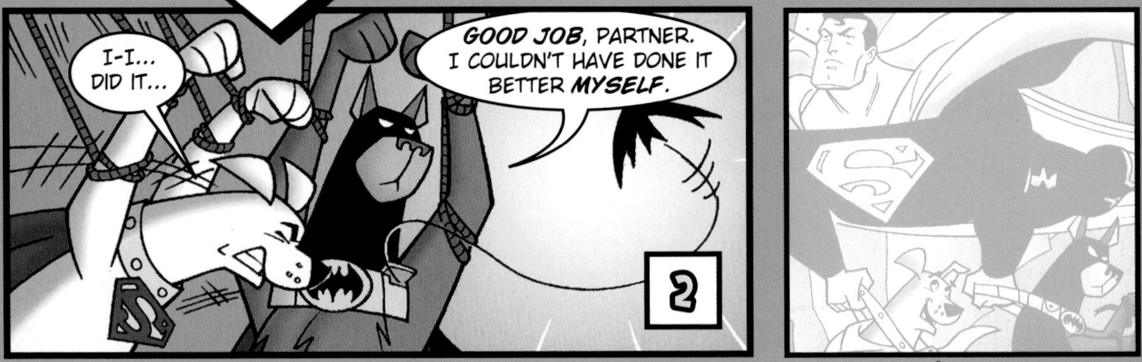
I-I... DID IT...
GOOD JOB, PARTNER. I COULDN'T HAVE DONE IT BETTER *MYSELF*.
2

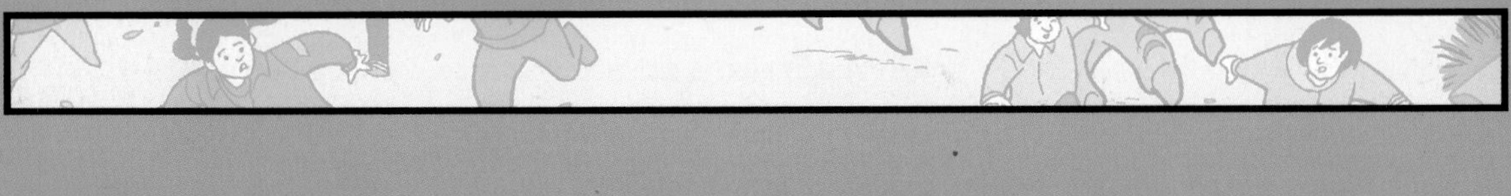

3. BASED ON WHAT YOU KNOW ABOUT KRYPTO, WHY DO YOU THINK WE CAN SEE THROUGH THE WALL IN THIS PANEL?

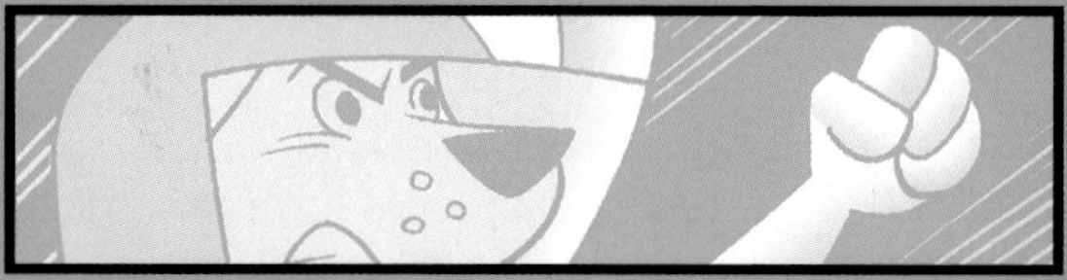

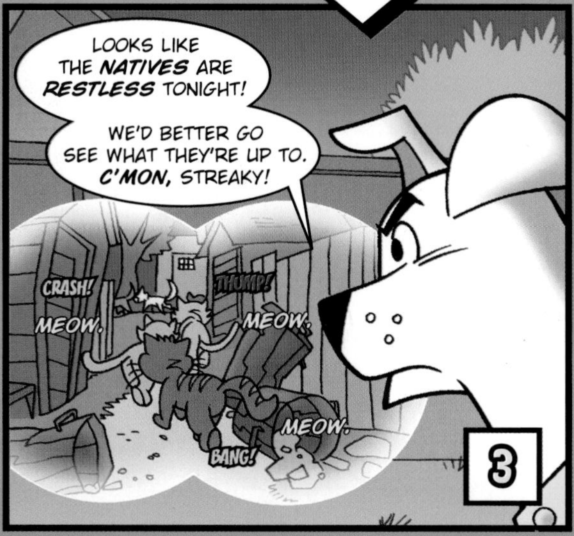
LOOKS LIKE THE *NATIVES* ARE *RESTLESS* TONIGHT!
WE'D BETTER GO SEE WHAT THEY'RE UP TO. *C'MON,* STREAKY!
CRASH!
THUMP!
MEOW.
MEOW.
MEOW.
BANG!
3

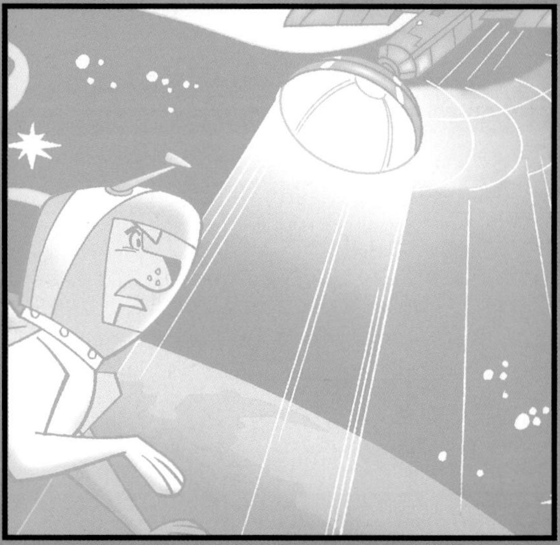

4. WADDLES CAN CREATE GREEN CONSTRUCTS WITH HIS MIND. DO YOU KNOW OF ANY OTHER COMICS CHARACTERS THAT CAN DO THIS? WHAT KINDS OF THINGS WOULD YOU CREATE IF YOU HAD THIS POWER?

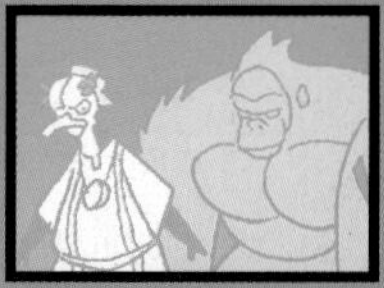

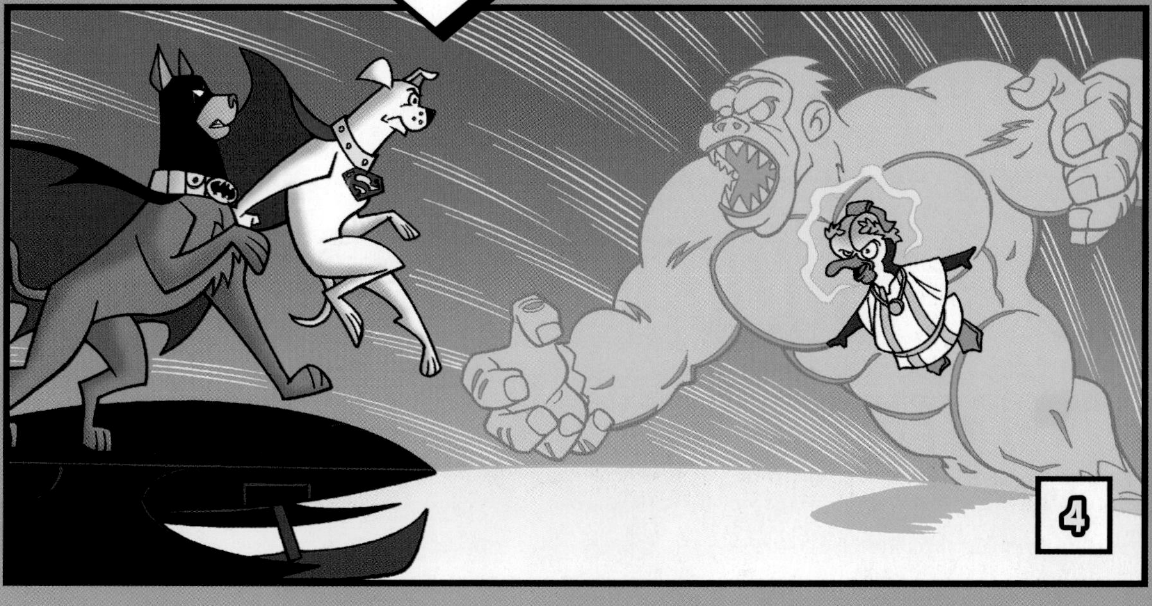
4

READ THEM ALL!

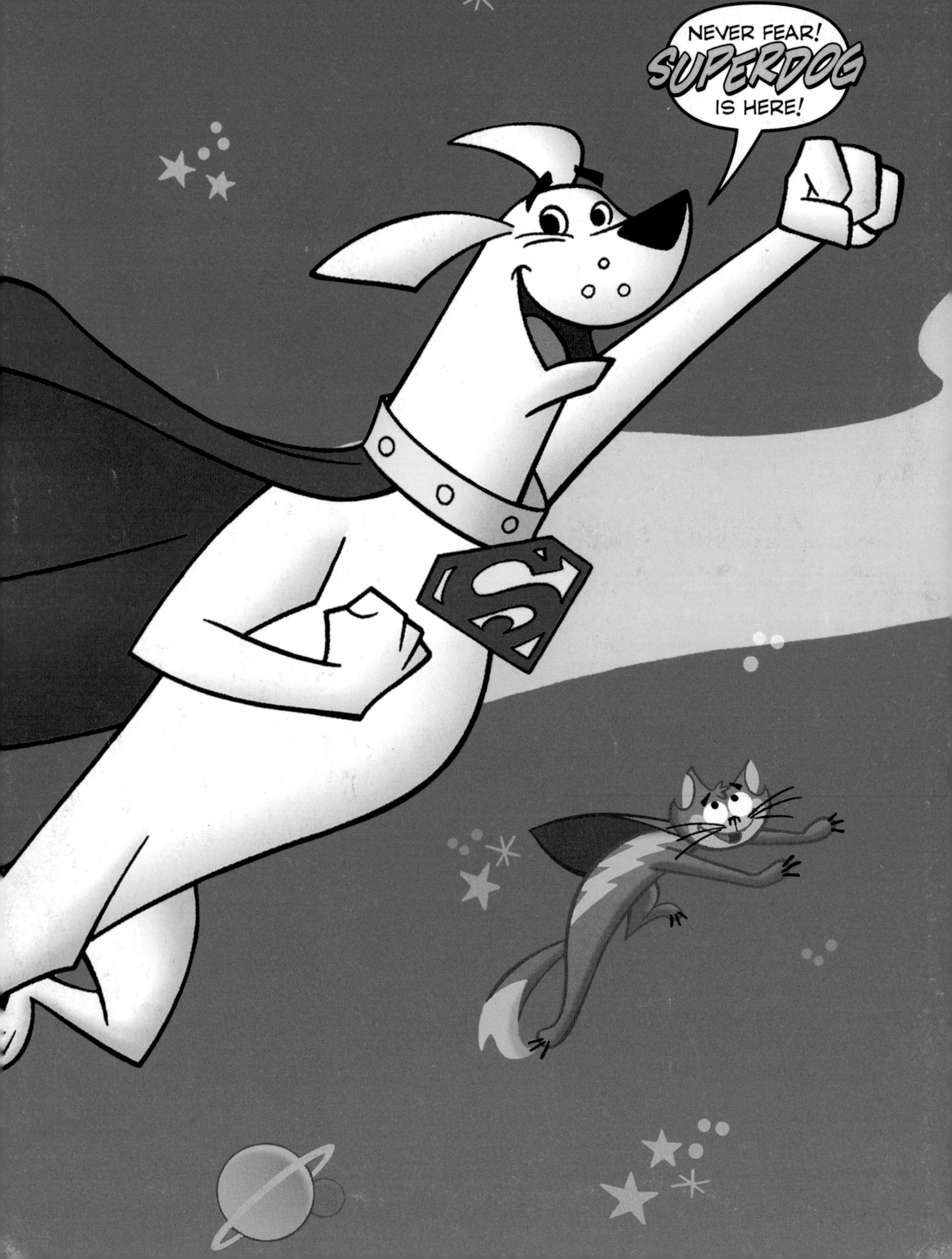
NEVER FEAR! SUPERDOG IS HERE!

KRYPTO
The SUPERDOG™

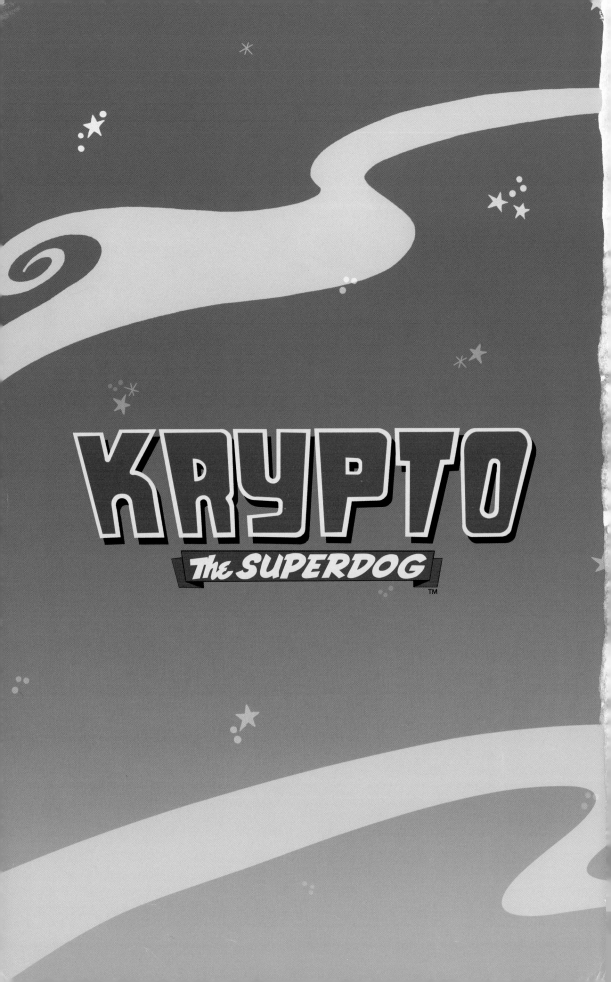

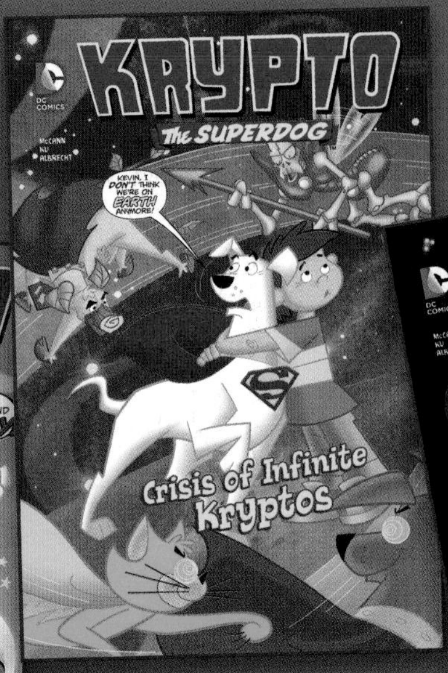
DC COMICS
KRYPTO
The SUPERDOG
McCANN
KU
ALBRECHT
KEVIN, I DON'T THINK WE'RE ON EARTH ANYMORE!
Crisis of Infinite Kryptos

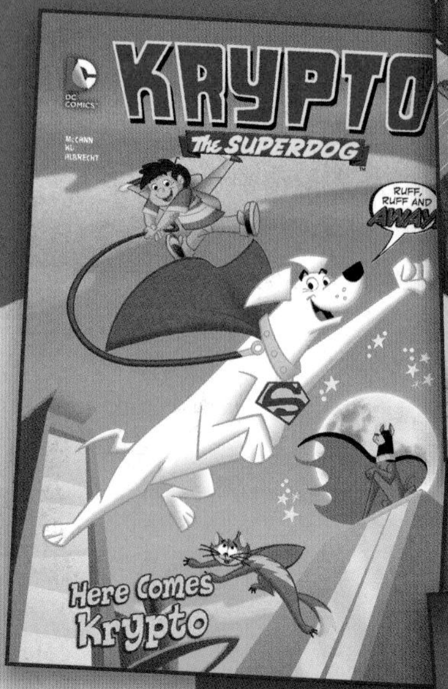
DC COMICS
KRYPTO
The SUPERDOG
McCANN
KU
ALBRECHT
RUFF, RUFF AND AWAY!
Here Comes Krypto

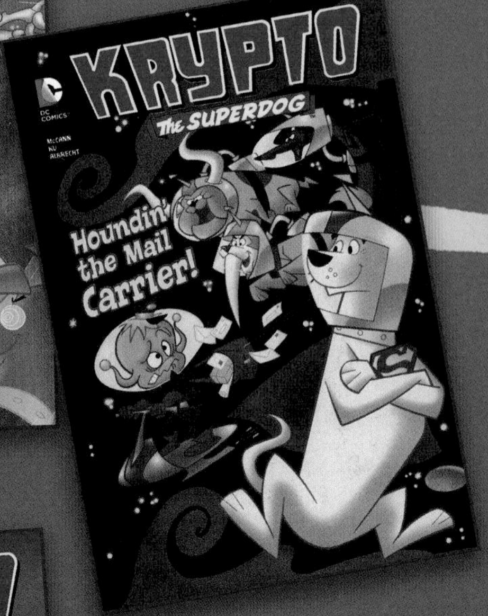
DC COMICS
KRYPTO
The SUPERDOG
McCANN
KU
ALBRECHT
Houndin' the Mail Carrier!

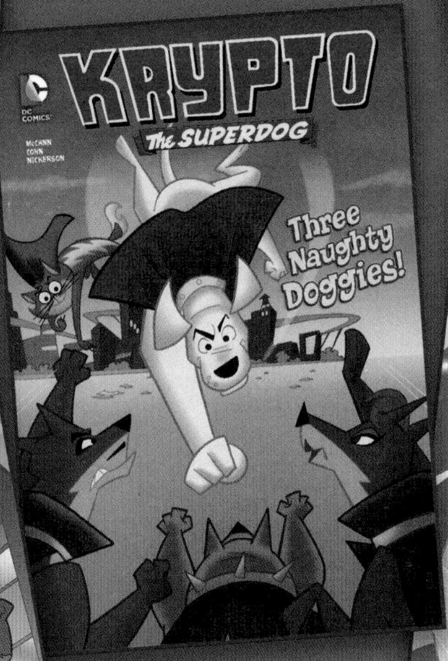
DC COMICS
KRYPTO
The SUPERDOG
McCANN
CONN
NICKERSON
Three Naughty Doggies!

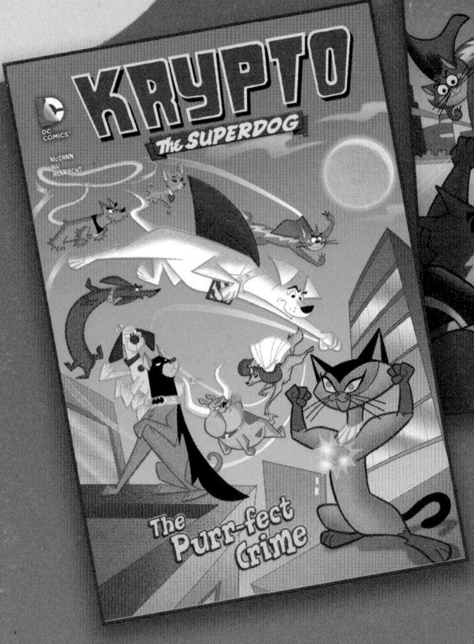
DC COMICS
KRYPTO
The SUPERDOG
McCANN
KU
ALBRECHT
The Purr-fect Crime

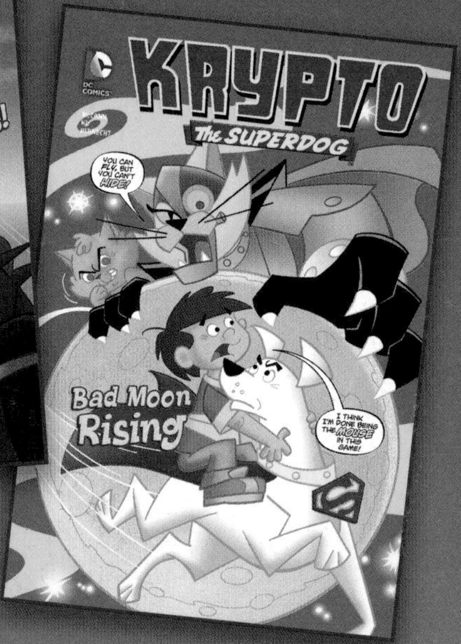
DC COMICS
KRYPTO
The SUPERDOG
YOU CAN FLY, BUT YOU CAN'T HIDE!
Bad Moon Rising
I THINK I'M DONE BEING THE MOUSE IN THIS GAME!

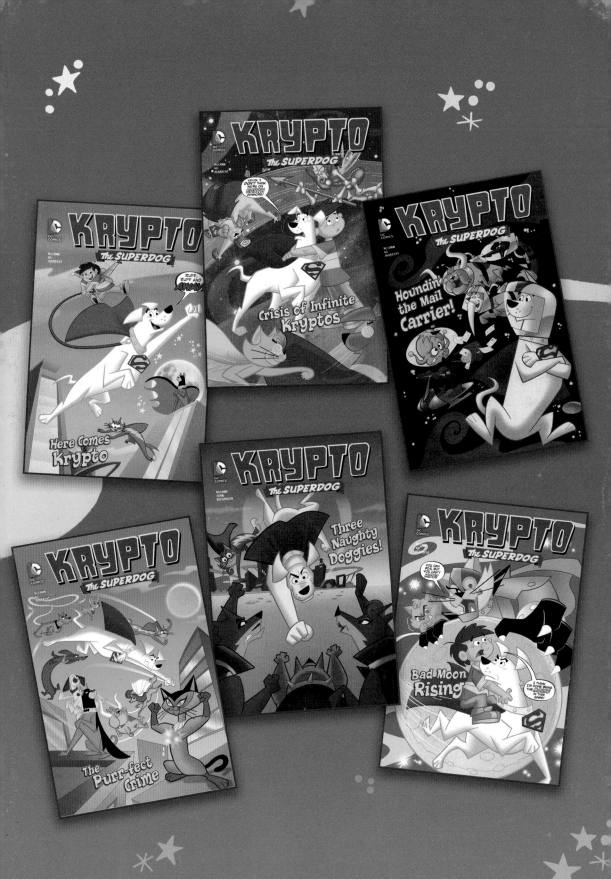

only from...

STONE ARCH BOOKS™